ADVANCE PRAISE FOR
Meet the Sky

"*Meet the Sky* is a heartfelt, heart-pounding look at weathering all of life's many storms—a story about strength, difficult choices, second chances, and the power of forgiveness. Sophie is highly relatable and deeply honest, and her beloved—yet treacherous—North Carolina barrier islands are beautifully evoked."

Kelly Loy Gilbert, author of *Picture Us in the Light*

"In every hurricane, there is an eye, and in every McCall Hoyle book, there is a core of deep emotion. With effervescent prose and vivid characters, *Meet the Sky* is a sweeping tale of unwavering hope in the face of a relentless storm."

Pintip Dunn, *New York Times* bestselling author of YA fiction, 2016 RWA RITA winner for Best First Book, and 2018 RITA finalist for Best Young Adult Romance

"*Meet the Sky* is an endearing story about how love can help us weather the storms of life."

Katie McGarry, acclaimed author of *Breathe*

"Sophie and Finn will take your heart by storm! A suspenseful story about the power of nature and two teens learning to live and love in an uncertain world."

Amy Fellner Dominy, award-winning author of *The Fall of Grace*

"McCall Hoyle's *Meet the Sky* is a story of survival, courage, and love. Compelling and wonderfully written, it will resonate with readers seeking a protagonist who is selfless and resourceful, forced to battle a setting both beautiful and brutal. This book is not to be missed!"

"Against the stunning backdrop of the Outer Banks mid-hurricane, complete with wild horses and even wilder winds, McCall Hoyle turns grief into something beautiful. *Meet the Sky* is a story about broken families trying to put the pieces of their fractured lives back together. Sophie and Finn prove what it means to forge ahead against all odds, even in the eye of a storm."

"*Meet the Sky* is a beautifully crafted story about grief, love, and the power of tragedy to shift our perspective on life. The character's realistic struggle through a deadly hurricane will have you devouring the pages! A perfect summer read."

"A riveting story about the quest to find safety and survival, and also the things we stay alive for: friendship, family, and love."

"A turbulent and emotionally-charged tale of survival, hope, and second chances. *Meet the Sky* is a beautiful testament to the only thing more powerful than nature—the resilience of the human spirit."

"In *Meet the Sky*, McCall Hoyle weaves a lyrical tapestry of beauty in the midst of devastation. A moving reminder of the importance of seizing every moment with the people we love."

Kate Watson, Foreword INDIE Award
finalist and author of *Seeking Mansfield*

"McCall Hoyle does it again! She weaves a tale that leaves us clinging to hope, courage, perseverance, family, and love. *Meet the Sky* is a beautiful story of standing strong in the path of extremes—in the eye of the hurricane, in the eye of the human condition."

Mary Rand Hess, bestselling author of *Solo*

"With tension splashed on every page, Hoyle takes her readers—and characters—on an emotional journey that will keep them up all night, turning pages."

Christina June, author of *It Started with Goodbye* and *Everywhere You Want to Be*

"*Meet the Sky* is a wonderful story that dares to ask the question, 'Is it *really* better to have loved and lost than to have never loved at all?' Written with honesty, yet also full of sweetness and hope, this is a story that will touch readers' hearts and linger with them long after they have finished the book."

Stephanie Morrill, author of *The Lost Girl of Astor Street*

"A whirlwind of a story full of hope and second chances. Hoyle stuns with *Meet the Sky* and leaves us in raptures with her beautifully crafted tale."

Alison Gervais, author of *In 27 Days*

"*Meet the Sky* was a hurricane I wanted to stay stranded within! I was hooked in the first few pages and swept away until the end."

Becca Hamby, Tome Student Literacy Society

Other books by McCall Hoyle

The Thing with Feathers

Meet the Sky

McCall Hoyle

BLINK

BLINK

Meet the Sky
Copyright © 2018 by McCall Hoyle

Requests for information should be addressed to:
Blink, 3900 Sparks Dr. SE, Grand Rapids, Michigan 49546

Hardcover ISBN 978-0-310-76570-7

Audio download ISBN 978-0-310-76568-4

Ebook ISBN 978-0-310-76565-3

Cover design: Brand Navigation
Interior design: Denise Froehlich

Printed in the United States of America

18 19 20 21 22 / LSC / 10 9 8 7 6 5 4 3 2 1

To Dusty, who believes I can meet the sky, even when I don't always believe it myself.

On either side the river lie
Long fields of barley and of rye,
That clothe the wold and meet the sky;
And thro' the field the road runs by
    To many-tower'd Camelot;
And up and down the people go,
Gazing where the lilies blow
Round an island there below,
    The island of Shalott.

"The Lady of Shalott"
—Alfred, Lord Tennyson

CHAPTER ONE

So many worlds, so much to do,
so little done, such things to be.

ALFRED, LORD TENNYSON

Once upon a time, I believed in fairy tales. Not any-more. If Prince Charmings and happily-ever-afters were real, I'd have a godmother and a fancy dress. Instead, I've got a pitchfork and a pile of horse manure.

Don't get me wrong. I'm thankful for what I have. I'm thankful for the rumble of the incoming tide in the distance. I'm thankful to live on the barrier islands of North Carolina, which might be as close to heaven as anyone on earth will ever get. But I'm also realistic. I overslept this morning and have a tight schedule and five more stalls to clean before school. The smallest complication can knock my entire day out of whack, and when that happens, it affects the horses and what's left of my family. That's why I'm sprinting behind the bouncy wheel-barrow like I'm competing in some kind of *American Ninja* manure challenge.

"You okay, Mere?" I call over my shoulder as I dump the wheelbarrow full of dirty wood shavings on the manure pile.

"Yes," she answers from inside the barn. Her voice sounds the same as it always has. It's about the only thing in our lives that's still the same, though. This time last year, Meredith was applying to Ivy League colleges, helping me with the barn, and dancing her heart out. Since the accident, she's content binge watching *Full House* episodes and sitting alone in her room. Whether or not she believes it, she needs me. Mom needs me too.

And I will not complain. Ever.

Pushing my shoulders back, I drop the pitchfork into the empty wheelbarrow and march back up the little hill to the barn. Jack, the old sorrel gelding in the first stall, whinnies when I reach the concrete pad in front of the double doors. I need to keep moving. Any minute now Mere will have had enough. She'll be too hot or too tired and need to head back to the house. But I can't resist the old guy. He's been part of this family longer than I have.

Leaving the wheelbarrow in the middle of the aisle, I head to his stall. His ears perk up as I pull two carrots from the back pocket of my faded jeans. For just a second, his whiskered muzzle tickles my palm, and I forget the chores I need to finish before school. But not for long. When I glance out the opening at the back of his stall, the morning sun reflects off the dunes. It's going to be brutally hot in another hour. With a sigh, I give Jack a quick scratch under his forelock and return to the wheelbarrow.

I peek in at Mere each time I pass the tack room. She sits in a straight-back chair in front of a row of saddles and bridles. Her hands lie motionless in her lap as she stares at the blank wall in front of her. When I finish the fifth stall, I stand the wheelbarrow beside the pile of wood shavings at the back of the barn, then hang the pitchfork on the wall. Brushing my hands on my jeans, I head to Mere in the tack room and run through my mental checklist of assignments due today at school—an illustrated timeline for US History, annotations for English, and a translated paragraph for Spanish.

When my boots hit the hardwood floor, Mere blinks but doesn't move. "You okay?" I ask.

She shrugs.

I reach for her blonde braid to give it a gentle tug, but she slouches lower in her chair. I let my hand fall back to my side. Her thick hair reminds me of Dad's. She got his movie star good looks, complete with square white teeth and defined cheekbones. I, on the other hand, inherited more of Mom's girl-next-door vibe—pretty on a good day, but not startlingly so like Mere.

"Who colored that?" She points to a page torn from a coloring book that's pinned to the corkboard on the wall above the saddles.

"You did, with one of the tourist kids last year. Remember?" I shouldn't have said the *remember* part. She's sensitive about being forgetful.

Shaking my head, I try not to stare at the colorful picture. A little over a year ago, Mere colored every speck of the princess's skin neon green and her long hair violet. Pinned up beside the princess is a coloring page of a castle. I colored that one with the same little girl.

It had been raining that day, and Mere and I were supposed to entertain the kids of the family waiting to ride horses on the beach. The girl had painted the sky above the castle rosy pink. I'd colored the individual stones a bland gray and had never once gone outside the lines.

"I don't remember," Mere says, closing her eyes and resting her head against the back of the chair.

It's best just to let it go, so I don't say anything. I reach for her Pop-Tarts wrapper. "Let's pick up, okay?"

Mere nods and brushes a few crumbs from the table at her side to the floor. I double-check the latch on the feed cabinet before we head out. We can't afford a repeat of the mutant-mouse infiltration we experienced a few months ago—not with Mere's physical and occupational therapy bills stacking up on the kitchen counter. As I turn back to Mere, a cat brushes my leg and meows.

"Oh, Jim—" He stares up at me with pitiful eyes, balancing on his three good legs. His fourth leg hangs awkwardly above the floor. I doubt we'll ever figure out what took his paw. He waves the knobby leg at me when I don't move, clearly hoping I'll acknowledge his cuteness and whip out the cat treats.

Meow. "Come on, sweet boy." I lift the lightweight cat into the crook of one arm and scratch him under his orange chin. Mere finally gets up and walks over to nuzzle her cheek against Jim's. When he purrs, his whole body vibrates. He reaches toward Mere with his nub of an arm, and she and I both giggle.

I set him on the counter, then grab an empty bowl and the plastic tub of cat food from the overhead cabinet. When the first bit clinks the bottom of the metal bowl, he digs in.

"Okay, Mere, let's get you back to the house." I squeeze her hand and lead her toward the sandy hill that separates our house from the barn.

As we climb the steps to our cottage on stilts, I'm careful

to position myself behind her in case she misses a step. She holds on to the stair rail, carefully planting one foot and then the other on each step. It's hard to believe this is the same girl who literally pirouetted and plié-ed her way through life, that all that muscle coordination and grace could be ripped away in an instant.

I sigh as the sun rises off to the east over the Atlantic. Swirls of pink and orange mingle with the occasional wispy cloud, kissing the gray-blue water where they meet on the horizon. The brushstrokes of color take my breath away. They're almost beautiful enough to make me believe in fairy tales again.

Almost.

I wipe a bead of sweat from my forehead as I reach for the doorknob. Despite the colors whirling in the sky and the grumble of the distant surf, the air has been oddly still the last couple of days. There is no rustling of sea oats today, not even a hint of a breeze. And it's hot. And humid—unnaturally so, more like July than October.

"That was quick," Mom says as we enter the kitchen. She turns down the volume on the weather radio she's been listening to 24/7 since a tropical depression formed out in the Atlantic three days ago. As the screen door bangs shut behind us, I realize a wave of bacon-y goodness fills the kitchen.

"I used my super manure powers." I swoosh my arms back and forth, ninja style.

A faint smile lights her face as she stands perfectly still, her metal tongs hovering above the frying pan. Her small frame and light-brown ponytail are identical to mine. In fact, people used to confuse us for sisters. But now her skin has lost its healthy and youthful glow. My chest tightens at the sight of the furrows in her forehead, deep enough to grip a pencil.

"You're working too hard, Sophie. I wish we could afford to hire someone."

If Dad hadn't left, she wouldn't have to worry about me. Before the accident, Mom ran the business side of things—answered the phone, paid the pills, advertised on social media, even dealt with finicky customers looking to purchase once-in-a-lifetime memories for themselves and their children. With Dad gone, the place was going downhill—fast. I might be a manure master, even a veterinary technician in a pinch, but I wasn't that great with hammers or handiwork. Last year, we had tourists lined up months in advance. Now, people could show up unannounced and pretty much be guaranteed a ride.

When the grease in the pan pops, Mom and I both jump.

"I told you it's not a big deal. I've got it." Mere and I wash our hands at the sink, then I hand Mere a pillow from the nearby couch as I guide her toward the breakfast table. She grips it against her chest. Somehow squeezing an object against her core improves Mere's balance—something to do with centering or activating one side of her frontal lobe. Plus I think the velvety texture soothes her somehow.

Mom has good intentions with the whole let's-find-someone-to-help-around-the-barn project, but she's living in a dream world if she thinks anyone would shovel horse poop and haul hay bales for what we could afford to pay anytime in the near future.

"Someone moved into the cottage near the dunes," she says as she flips a piece of bacon.

"Mmm hmmm." I grab three plastic cups and a carton of OJ from the fridge and head back to the table.

Mere smiles when I approach. I unfold the cardboard spout and fill her cup.

"I'm pretty sure it's the same family that used to live there. What was their name?"

My hand jerks. Juice splashes Mere's arm, and she gasps. Mom turns around to see what happened.

"You okay?" she asks.

"Uh, yeah."

I scurry toward the sink for a towel. I'm being silly. First, it's probably not the same family. Second, even if it is, it's not a big deal. So what if I had the crush-to-end-all-crushes on Finn Sanders. So what if he said he'd meet me at homecoming and didn't show. It was freshman year. It was a crush. It wasn't like we were together or anything. It wasn't even a real date. But it was still humiliating. Yesenia and a couple of other girls came over to my house ahead of time. Mere did our hair and makeup. They were as excited as I was. Then he didn't show, and I spent the night acting like I didn't care.

Even if it is Finn, he and I have no reason to interact or cross paths now. We became friends in middle school when we were dumped into the morning chess club together; the school had to do something with us since our moms dropped us off so early. Finn and I became obsessed with beating each other and with putting our heads together to beat Mr. Jackson and his Dutch Defense. It was surprisingly fun. But that was years ago. I can't even remember the last time I played chess or thought about Finn.

"I just drew a blank. What was the boy's name? Jeff?" Mom lays the last slice of bacon on a paper plate to drain.

"Finn. His name's Finn." I dab Mere's placemat and arm with the towel while she hums a piece of music she danced to a couple of years ago.

"That's right—Finn. Maybe he'd like to earn a few dollars helping around the barn." She brings the bacon and a plate of blackened toast to the table, and I do my best not to sigh.

"I've got it, Mom. I promise." I try not to sound concerned as I slide into my seat and reach for a piece of toast. I really don't want her asking me why I'm not eating, but suddenly a flock of seagulls is swarming in my belly.

"Something will work out. It has to. You can't keep going like this." She pushes the plate of bacon toward me.

She's the one who can't keep going like this. But instead of arguing with her, I bite into my dry toast and try to swallow my feelings.

"I bet you'll see Finn today. You could ask him about it."

Or not.

My throat tightens around the single bite of toast as I twist my lips into a smile and check the time on my phone. I have precisely twelve minutes if I'm going to leave on time.

I may not be able to leave home a year early for college like we'd planned. I may not be able to follow my dreams of veterinary medicine. But I can control one thing. I can control whether I talk to Finn Sanders.

And let me assure you, there won't be conversation or anything else going on between us.

CHAPTER TWO

My mind is clouded with a doubt.

ALFRED, LORD TENNYSON

I make it to seventh period without any drama and without any run-ins with Finn, so the optimistic part of me, the part I've squashed down recently, starts to believe maybe Mom was wrong about the whole Finn thing. Besides, I love seventh period. It's technically a study hall, but it's the one hour in the day that's completely mine. No chores. Nobody counting on me. It's pretty much my hour to do whatever I want, and I normally spend it in the media center with Yesenia. She and I have been best friends for as long as I can remember. We're perfect together. I'm a good listener. She's a good talker. It's a win-win.

Mrs. Hampson, the librarian, nods as I pass, but her eyes remain locked on the TV mounted above the checkout desk. Even with the sound muted, it's obvious the meteorologist is taking the weather seriously. His face is grim as he points to the kaleidoscope of green, blue, and yellow on the radar map that's starting to resemble a spiral of colorful soft-serve ice cream.

I head to the overstuffed leather chairs near a big wall of windows to wait for Yesenia and check my phone to make sure I don't miss any notifications about my schedule, or

Mom's, or Mere's. The view of the dunes out back calms my nerves even though they remind me of Dad. He loved those dunes. Mere and I spent much of our childhood exploring them with him.

"Scout," he'd call to me over the wind, "chart your own course." He loved that I was brave enough to charge up one side of a dune and down the other without him.

As the waves of heat shimmer and bake the sand, I wonder what happened to that gutsy little Sophie. It's like she died in the accident. Or is she still inside me somewhere, like the mountains of sand in the distance that constantly shift and change but never actually blow away? I don't know anymore. Right this minute, though, I'm content to admire the dunes in the distance.

For the first time today, I breathe—really breathe—and open my tattered collection of Alfred, Lord Tennyson poems we're reading for English. Yesenia's familiar footsteps interrupt me on page three. When I look up, she huffs and plops her army-green bag on the floor beside the chair facing me. Her favorite patch—*half Mexican, half American, completely Awesome*—dangles from a few loose threads.

"You heard, right?" She leans toward me, her eyes wide. Locks of thick black hair bounce around her face.

I fold down my page and play dumb as my earlier optimism fades. "Heard what?"

"He's back," she hisses, trying to avoid the wrath of Mrs. Hampson. "And he starts classes tomorrow."

"Who's back?" I ask, but the rocks in my stomach tell me I already know.

"Finn Sanders." She pauses, waiting for the news to settle.

"He's supposed to be hot and some kind of supersurfer now. And he's in all advanced classes."

I force down the lump in my throat. If he's in all advanced classes, we're going to have almost the same exact schedule. "It's not a big deal—really. He and I never had anything in common."

She lifts a finger and points teasingly at my face. Her brown eyes reflect the sunlight streaming in through the bank of windows. "What about chess?"

I smirk and tilt my head. "Haven't played in months."

She narrows her eyes. "Science fair?"

I swipe at a strand of hair that defiantly refuses to remain braided and cross my arms. "Didn't compete last year."

She switches tactics. "I think it's romantic, like a reunion. You know what I always say about fate—"

"Yes." Yesenia has a saying for everything, and I adore her. But sometimes her glass-is-always-overflowing outlook gets us both in trouble. In sixth grade, when I still believed in imaginary lands and magical creatures, she talked me into writing a play and spending all our Christmas money on props and costumes. We didn't sell any tickets and had nothing to show for our Christmas cash. In eighth grade, her school spirit ended up getting us sent home for the day to wash our neon green Cindy Lou Who hair. And if I remember correctly, she was the one who encouraged me in ninth grade to "go after Finn Sanders."

She barrels on anyway. "And you *did* have a lot in common. You two were always competing."

"We weren't."

"Ummm, yes, you were. There was the Humane Society fund-raising contest—"

Thankfully, she's interrupted by Emilie, a relatively new member of our junior class who also managed to score a free seventh period. She has a seizure response dog because of her epilepsy, and she hangs out with him in the media center most afternoons. He's gorgeous, with a big, blocky golden retriever head and sheets of feathery blond hair on his chest, legs, and tail. The moment I met him, I loved him—though to be fair, I love pretty much every dog I meet. Okay, I pretty much like all the cats and guinea pigs and baby goats too.

"Hey, Hitch." I pat my leg in invitation.

He glances up at Emilie, hopeful.

"Free," she says, and he ambles over to rest his head on my lap.

I give him a good scratch behind the ears and lean down to rub my face against his. Before my family fell to pieces, I had a plan. I'd graduate a year early and head to State for my veterinary degree. Even though vet school is extremely competitive, I knew I would almost certainly get in. I've been around animals since the day I was born, and other than Yesenia, animals tend to be my best friends. Doc Wiggins, the vet who cares for our horses, graduated from State and promised me a great reference, and my parents are known for their work protecting and rescuing wild horses on the Outer Banks. They even built a fence that spans the entire island and keeps the wild horses safe from the people and buildings that continue to encroach on their habitat. I dreamed of working with animals like Hitch and little Jim every day and of living happily ever after.

Then everything changed with one tick of the second hand, and I learned an important lesson. Actually, I learned several important lessons—be alert, protect what you love, and maintain control of what you can at all costs.

That's what I do. And it's working.

"Do y'all think we'll have to evacuate?" Emilie asks, interrupting my thoughts.

I snap to attention, my hands freezing on Hitch's ears. "Evacuate?"

"Yeah, the weather service announced that the tropical depression is now officially Hurricane Harry." She touches her leg. Without a second's hesitation, Hitch pads to her side. "My mom will want to leave tomorrow to beat any rush."

"We won't go unless there's a mandatory evacuation," Yesenia says with a shrug. Like most people living on the Outer Banks, she's no stranger to storms. But I get why Emilie and her mom have to be careful—Emilie has to have access to 911 and the hospital across the bridge if she seizes.

I miss what they say next. I'm thinking about Mom, Mere, the horses, and Jim, and how this could be a false alarm. We won't evacuate unless it's a mandatory evacuation either. It takes a tremendous amount of time and work to get the horses off the island, and it's expensive to board them on the mainland until the storm dies down. We have to be careful because of money—or the lack of it. That's why I've had to put college on hold—unless I get a full ride to State, we can't afford it, and even if I did get a scholarship, Mom and Mere couldn't keep the barn going without me. That barn is what keeps the roof over our heads and dinner on the table.

The librarian gives us the stink eye, so Emilie and Hitch head toward their standard spot near the biographies. Yesenia spends the rest of the period working on her math homework, though I can feel her glancing at me from time to time like she wants to say more about Finn. I manage to read a few more pages of Tennyson.

When the bell rings, releasing us from seventh period, I've put the Finn conversation behind me. Yesenia and I swing by my locker on our way out of the building, and I grab the poetry anthology Mr. Richards has required for next semester. If I have any time before bed, I might get a jumpstart on annotating. I'll be lucky to scrounge up enough time and money in the next year and a half to sneak away to the community college a few days a week, but that doesn't mean I'll let my grades slip.

"Really?" Yesenia asks with a laugh when she sees me put the book in my bag. "We don't have to read that until January."

"I know," I tell her, sheepish. "I can't help myself."

As we push through the double doors and step outside, the heat smacks us in the face. Our sandals scuff the sandy sidewalk as we stroll toward the parking lot. There's no reason to hurry. One thing all Southerners know is how to match their pace to the ninety-plus degrees and one hundred percent humidity without breaking a sweat.

Yesenia points at a dance banner tied to the chain-link fence by the parking lot. "Don't forget about the dance next week."

Shifting my heavy backpack from one shoulder to the other, I nod and keep moving.

"What?" she asks.

"Nothing."

She grabs the sleeve of my T-shirt, stopping me in my tracks and leveling her eyes on me. "Don't you dare think about bailing on me."

I scan the parking lot for my battered truck, avoiding her gaze. "I'm not bailing on you. Promise." I force a half smile.

"Okay." She doesn't sound convinced. "Because you promised. This is supposed to be our year to live. Have fun being in high school before next year, when we'll be totally stressed about college applications. We're upperclassmen now. Remember?"

"I remember," I say, scrolling through the mental list of things I need to do after school.

"Good. You also remember our motto, right?" she asks when we reach the truck.

I open the driver's door and step up onto the running board. "Yeah, shoot for the moon. Even if you miss, you'll—"

"No, not that one." She tosses her bag on the floor and climbs into the passenger seat in one fluid movement. "The Tennyson quote."

We snap on our seat belts, and, holding my breath, I turn the key in the ignition. One day my family will have dependable vehicles with new tires and engines that don't leak oil. Not today. Today it's just me and Mom, still trying to recover from the accident that wrecked my parents' marriage and ruined Mere's future. When the engine roars to life, I exhale, thankful to have dodged a possible crisis. Then we turn out of the parking lot, and I tighten my grip on the wheel. Ever since Mere and Dad's accident, I see danger around every turn and around every vehicle within a quarter mile radius of my bumper.

"You know," Yesenia says when I don't respond. "*'Tis better to have loved and lost than never to have loved at all.'*"

I study oncoming traffic as I try not to roll my eyes. There's no point in arguing with her. She's never lost anything, not even a pet, and certainly not half of her family. She believes Tennyson.

I happen to know better.

It's way worse to love and lose than to play it safe and miss the heartbreak altogether. Yesenia can have Tennyson's pretty words. Personally, I'm more of a don't-count-your-chickens-before-they-hatch kind of girl.

As we creep along the beach road, Yesenia unzips her bag and pulls out a battered composition book. I know what's inside—the high school bucket list she's been working on since freshman year.

"The love doesn't just have to do with guys, you know," Yesenia reminds me as she flips the pages. "It's about loving *life*, or at least taking an occasional risk."

"Uh-huh," I reply. We've had this conversation a million times, but I remain unconvinced that taking a risk—any risk—is a good thing. When a gust of wind rocks the truck, I ease my foot off the brake and tighten my grip on the steering wheel. The cedar-sided shacks to our right balance on wisps of sand too small to be called actual dunes. It's a wonder the breeze doesn't wash them out to sea.

"Which is why we have a lot to accomplish in the next two years." Yesenia starts reading from her list. "Hang glide, go on a cruise, skinny-dip, invite dates to the Sadie Hawkins dance—"

"Invite dates?"

"What? That's been on there for ages. You don't listen, Sophie."

"I always listen. It's just the list is always growing. It's hard to keep track. You said, 'go to dance.' I don't remember anything about *inviting* someone." I mean, I know the whole purpose of a Sadie Hawkins dance is that girls do the inviting, but still. I try to formulate an argument about living in a feminist society where we don't need Sadie Hawkins dances in the first place, but Yesenia is still reading.

"Build a snowman—I know it's impractical at the beach, but still—enter hot dog eating contest, learn to play the ukulele, eat caviar—"

"I don't remember any of those." I glance in my side and rearview mirrors as I prepare to flick my turn signal. A blob of green barrels up behind me, practically kissing my bumper.

"A few of those might be new, but . . ." She trails off as I tap my brakes and looks behind us. "What is that guy doing?"

A vomit-green Chevy Blazer whips around us despite the double yellow line and flies past my driver's side window. The car or truck or whatever it is has larger rust patches than mine. I hold the steering wheel tight and train my eyes straight ahead, braking as quickly as I can. My heart pounds in my chest, a rapid, harsh rhythm that makes me feel faint.

Yesenia jabs my shoulder, laughing.

"Stop," I squeal. "We're about to die."

"No, we're not. That was Finn. And he looks good—really good." She fans herself as he drives on, leaving us in a cloud of exhaust and sand.

I pull over to the edge of the road to rest my head on the steering wheel and make sure I'm not really having a heart attack. "I . . . I . . . That jerk. He's going to kill someone. He shouldn't be allowed to drive."

"But he looks good behind the wheel."

"Stop, Yesenia. It's not funny. He could have hurt us. My brakes aren't all that reliable, and I really need new tires." As if to prove my point, my back tire spins, kicking up sand before gaining enough traction to move back onto the road.

"I doubt they're that bad," she says. "Your mom wouldn't let you drive if the truck wasn't safe."

"She doesn't know. She's got too many bills to worry about already. And if a storm is really coming, shutting down business this weekend won't help either. For some reason, people don't want to horseback ride on the beach with a hurricane coming."

"You should tell her if the truck is that bad." For once, Yesenia sounds serious.

"No. I'll have enough tip money in a week or two—if some idiot reckless driver doesn't kill me first."

When we pull into her driveway a few minutes later, she smiles and reaches for the door handle.

"Be safe. Call me later," she says, then hops out of the truck.

I wave. Yesenia blows me a kiss and races up the steps of her house two at a time with her backpack thrown over one shoulder. Despite her never-ending desire to push me out of my comfort zone, she really is the best kind of friend. I know all that bucket-list stuff is more for me than for her, that it's Yesenia's way of wanting to help me get past all the crap that happened last year. Even though it's never going to work, I love her for trying.

Heading north with the ocean on my right, I catch an occasional glimpse of the rising tide between gaps in the dunes. I tell myself the waves are no higher than usual. Even if they are, that proves absolutely nothing. Higher waves could mean a tropical storm, a nor'easter, a false alarm, or even just a full moon. Nine times out of ten, all the hurricane hype is for nothing.

The hardware stores sell out of plywood and batteries. The gas stations might even run out of gas before an evacuation. Then more often than not, the hurricane turns back out to sea or just dissipates to a bad thunderstorm.

As I get closer to home, I ignore the cottage on the dunes near our house and the green Blazer in front of it. I flick my turn signal and pull into my driveway.

When I cut the engine, I tilt my head back and pray Finn will stay away.

CHAPTER THREE

O earth, what changes hast thou seen!

ALFRED, LORD TENNYSON

Mom and I have an after-dinner dishwashing routine. She scrapes plates and washes. I dry and put away. Mere and Jim cuddle on the couch under an old quilt as I slip the last chipped plate into a cabinet. Outside the window, the sea oats swish and swirl, signaling a break in the fierce heat, or at least a break in the eerie stillness of the last few days. The early evening sun casts rays of golden light on the trembling seed heads.

Mom's bare feet pad the wood floor as she heads to her spot at the end of the couch. I give the counters a quick wipe, trying to remember if she's wearing the same clothes she had on yesterday. I add laundry to my to-do list.

"You want to play checkers?" Mom asks as she settles into the worn cushions. I can see the exhaustion on her face, but I also know she'll do anything to draw Mere out of herself and into the world with us.

Glancing at the clock, I realize we have over an hour until dark. "I have a better idea," I say.

"Better than checkers?" Mom looks skeptical. Checkers

is one of the few activities that draws Mere out of her shell. Something about the rhythm of the game and the consistency of the red and black squares seems to organize her thinking. Sometimes she seems almost herself when we play checkers.

"We're going for a ride on the beach." I nod confidently as if it's a well-thought-out idea as opposed to a spur-of-the-moment plan to give Mom a break for an hour or so.

Mere tosses off the quilt, stands up, and grins, showing more emotion than I've seen from her in days. Poor Jim barely gets his three good legs under him before he slips to the floor, tangled in the quilt. But when Mom taps her thigh, he jumps into her lap, completely unfazed. He seems to smile and purrs as she runs her hand down his arched back. She smiles too as he kneads her faded leggings with his one good paw and his little nub.

Then Mom looks at me. "I thought you had homework." Her smile falters.

"It wasn't as much as I thought." I step around the table and pull Mere gently toward the hall leading to our bedrooms.

"Give me two minutes to grab my boots," Mere says, proving she's interested in the ride.

I duck into my room for my soft Justin Ropers, glad I suggested getting out of the house and onto the beach. Even though Mere may not think about it consciously, I believe the dancer in her likes the movement of the horse beneath her.

In a few minutes, we're out the door and almost to the barn. Mere walks ahead of me, then pauses to turn around with her arms spread wide. It's not exactly a *croisé devant*, but it's something. A light wind lifts her hair, and I smile. As we approach the breezeway of the barn, Jack nickers a soft greeting.

"I want to ride Roxie," Mere says as we step onto the concrete aisle. Hay particles hang suspended in slanted rays of sunlight—gold and amber with the occasional speck of ruby.

"But Jack will get his feelings hurt. And he didn't get out today." Roxie was Mere's before the accident, but she'll never ride her again. The mare's high-strung. If Jack has the even temper of a master yogi, Roxie is his polar opposite—whatever that might be. Her moods change like the wind.

"You ride Jack. I'll ride Dolly. They like to be together," I say. They're also guaranteed not to shy away from anything or cause any uncertain movement that might unseat Mere.

Jack and Dolly are Mom and Dad's original pair of trail horses. They're both mixed breeds, combining the intelligence and athleticism of their quarter horse dams with the calm nature and immense strength of their Clydesdale sires. The Clydesdale genes make them sturdy enough to carry even the most out-of-shape tourists through soft sand. They also have wider ribs and broader backs, perfect for riders like Mere who don't have good balance.

"Whatever." Mere's jaw twitches like she's contemplating arguing. Dolly shakes her mane, distracting her, and Mere seems to forget which horse she wanted to ride. She turns back to Dolly, humming quietly as she brushes her long gray neck while I saddle and bridle Jack. In no time, we're moving along the marked path over the dunes. The horses know the drill. Their hooves *shish-shish* rhythmically through the sand. The receding tide whispers to us—*whish, thump, whoosh*—as the low waves approach, break, and then recede.

With my lungs full of warm, salty air, there's less room for stress or worry.

"Look! Look!" Mere stands up in her saddle, pointing out to sea. Jack's ears flick back and forth between the flock of screaming, dive-bombing seagulls up ahead to the excited girl on his back.

"Easy, Jack," I soothe. His ears flick in my direction, his head dropping back to a more relaxed position. On autopilot, the horses plod toward the firmer sand near the water.

"Whoa, girl," I say to Dolly when a dolphin erupts from the frothy water beneath the gulls. Jack stops without instruction from Mere.

The dolphins have multiplied, and they're showing off like they know they have an audience. They take turns breaching, jumping clear of the water, then diving. They disappear for a minute, then emerge in perfect unison nose-first ahead of an incoming wave. They wear smiles beneath their bottlenoses as they head south, whistling and squeaking. Their enthusiasm is contagious.

I click my tongue on the roof of my mouth, instructing Dolly and Jack to move along. The temperature drops a degree or two, and the wind picks up half a notch as the horses clomp into the shallow surf. Even old Jack and Dolly seem to have a bit more spring in their steps.

"You want to race?" I ask.

Mere looks at me as if I've been inhabited by an alien.

"Really?" she asks.

"Really." I bounce my heels against Dolly's sides. She picks up the pace. Jack breaks into a bouncy trot.

"Use one leg," I call over the rush of wind and waves, hoping Jack will lope for Mere. We've been riding since we were three, but Mere's lack of coordination makes even the most natural commands difficult to carry out. Jack's trot is so jarring, there's no way she can stay balanced for long, but his lope is like sitting in a rocking chair. She could probably handle that for hours.

I lift my right heel into Dolly's ribs. She immediately leads off with her left foreleg, transitioning smoothly from a walk to the rolling one-two-three, one-two-three loping rhythm I could sit all day. Dolly takes the bit in her mouth and pulls steadily on the reins, clearly ready to show old Jack what she's got. I apply just enough pressure to ensure her nose stays behind Mere's thigh.

"I'm going to get you!" I say, teasing as we near the pier. Out here with the dolphins, and the wind, and the horses, I feel a tiny glimmer of my old self and tilt my face to the sky to soak up every last morsel of this feeling, wishing it could last forever.

"No way!" Mere pushes Jack harder.

He lumbers on ahead of me. Sitting deep in the saddle, I drop my heel, lengthen my calf, and ask Dolly to walk with my seat. She slows without any verbal command.

"You win, Mere. Jack, walk—easy," I command. He obeys.

"A little farther?" Mere twists in her saddle, her cheeks rosy.

"It's time to head back." And it is. I'd love to ride with Mere forever, but I need to study for an AP US History quiz. And Mere's moodiness is aggravated when she stays up too late.

I let her lead the way home. We ride in silence. The sea lulls my senses; it's the one constant in my life, despite all the changes of the last year. A year ago, Mere was the real leader, the role model, the big sister.

Then everything changed.

Now we pretend.

CHAPTER FOUR

I must lose myself in action,
lest I wither in despair.

ALFRED, LORD TENNYSON

Somehow, I don't pass out when I see Finn on the way into school the next morning. It helps that he's distracted by whatever's playing through his earbuds. When our eyes meet, he opens his mouth like he's about to speak. His chin lifts, and his eyelids drop a bit, masking what I seem to remember are green eyes.

Okay, I totally remember. They're precisely the same shade of dark green as the pine trees on the mainland. His hair is still jet black. But I forgot how big his nose is and how the hook of it is somehow attractive. A nose that prominent would make most guys self-conscious, but he wears it like a symbol of greatness.

I give a quick nod and pick up the pace so he can't see my face or the red splotches of heat I feel traveling from my neck to my ears. His flip-flops slap the concrete as we approach the breezeway. I keep moving, silently cursing Yesenia for catching the bus and leaving me to navigate this situation alone.

"Long time, no see, Bookworm." He bumps my arm with his elbow, forcing me to slow down and acknowledge him and his favorite nickname for me in eighth grade.

"Yeah. Long time." I shrug, sounding way cooler than I feel. "Sorry. I'm kind of in a hurry."

"After school, then?"

I glance at the time on my phone, scrambling for an excuse. "I have a tutoring session for math."

Unable to meet his eyes, I stare at the stubble on his chin, a reminder of how much older we are now.

"I just thought you might want to play." He wiggles his eyebrows and reaches in the back pocket of the jeans that hang at a perfect angle around his narrow hips. His long fingers conceal whatever he retrieved from his pocket. My face goes from warm to blazing. He's toying with me, I know, but I'm two steps behind and don't know where this is headed.

"I don't have time to . . . uh . . . *play*." I nod and scurry forward to open the door for a girl on crutches.

"I'll let you be white." He waves a small metal box in front of my face.

"What are you—" I'm thankful for my firm grip on the heavy door.

"I promise not to open with the Sicilian Defense. I remember how you hate that." He braces his hand on the door above my head and motions for me to enter ahead of him.

I blink at him. The fog in my head clears as I pass under his arm. He's talking about chess. The small box he was waving in my face is the same magnetic travel chess set he carried in his pocket in middle school. I almost laugh, but I don't want to encourage him.

"I don't play anymore." I glance at my phone again. This time I see a text from Mom, telling me to check the weather forecast.

"But you—"

"I've gotta go." I point at my phone and duck toward the science hall.

"Okay . . ."

I can't be certain, but I'm pretty sure his goofy I'm-too-cool-to-care grin wavers for a second. Without pausing to verify, I lift my hand in a weak farewell and scurry to safety. Halfway down the hall, I risk a quick glance over my shoulder. Finn's gone. I exhale slowly and detour to the girls' bathroom to catch my breath.

I make it through math without talking to Finn again. Even in fourth period, when Mr. Richards assigns him the seat directly behind me, I don't turn around to ask him how the past two years have been. I touch my finger to the jagged initials carved in the top of my desk, willing myself to focus on the day's lecture. But the part of my brain that's supposed to be analyzing the poem on the board constantly jumps to the barn and home.

The National Weather Service alert about the approaching storm doesn't scare me. Mom, on the other hand, has worked herself into a frenzy. She's texted me three times, asking me to check myself out for the day and come home. She doesn't care if I miss my Physics test. She says the horses are acting weird, and she trusts them way more than meteorologists or Doppler radar.

Mr. Richards doesn't seem to share my concerns, because his Robert Frost lecture has gone on without ceasing.

"Why does Frost say, 'Nature's first green is gold'?" he asks.

No one volunteers. No one moves. Maybe I wasn't the only one not paying attention.

Mr. Richards's eyes meet mine. He lifts one sparse eyebrow hopefully. "Sophie?"

I don't look away fast enough. He knows I'll have a decent answer, and he knows he can count on me to be respectful. I'm his go-to girl in a teaching pinch.

"Yeah, Sophie. Let's hear some scholarly analysis." Warm air brushes the back of my neck.

My teeth grate as I concentrate on not turning around. I know from middle school that acknowledging Finn will only encourage him, and I do not want to encourage him. The conversation this morning was enough interaction for the month. I swallow, lock eyes with Mr. Richards, and ignore the stare of the girl beside us who is obviously wondering why Finn is egging me on.

"Frost is using the metaphor to emphasize the precious nature of spring's first hint of green—of rebirth and renewal." I scoot to the front of my seat, trying to distance myself from Finn.

Mr. Richards nods, looking like he wants me to say more.

"You could say it's hyperbole and imagery too, and maybe even alliteration if you focus on the *green* and *gold*," I continue. It can't hurt to be nice to Mr. Richards. Maybe he'll remember my efforts on the essay portion of our next test.

A yawn breaks the stillness. Mr. Richards squints at someone in the back of the room. Then he does that teacher thing when he randomly calls on another unsuspecting soul to see if they're paying attention.

"What do you think, Mr. Sanders?"

Twenty-something heads swivel in Finn's direction. His presence may annoy me, but the rest of the class seems fascinated by his return. By the way everyone was laughing with him before the bell rang, he has slipped back into life at North Ridge without missing a beat. Finn may be smart, but he also loves to play class clown.

"Einstein here pretty much said it all." He flicks my ponytail with his pencil, clearly oblivious to the chilly vibes I've been sending his way all morning.

The people sitting near us chuckle. Not me. Finn starts to say more, but the intercom crackles overhead, and I breathe a sigh of relief, thanking God for the interruption.

The room goes silent. There's nothing like the threat of an oncoming hurricane, even a Category 1 storm, to get the attention of anyone who lives or works on the Outer Banks of North Carolina.

"Dare County Emergency Management has issued a mandatory evacuation to begin at nine o'clock tomorrow morning," our principal says. Even he sounds a little excited. Or nervous— it's hard to tell. "School will be canceled tomorrow and until the advisory expires."

Crap. Crap. Crap.

That means loading up the horses, locking up the barn and house, and racing to beat the evacuation madness. No one else in the room seems to care. When the room erupts in cheers, even Mr. Richards's face relaxes a bit.

"Sweet!" The kid at the front of my row fist pumps the air.

Someone mumbles something about a hurricane party and hunch punch. I don't want to care, but I can't help myself. Finn is less predictable than the weather. I'm curious to see how he will react, so I glance over my shoulder. I've heard rumors about his extreme surfing life in Virginia Beach, and some part of me wants to know how the fearless risk taker will react to the imminent threat of a hurricane.

Shockingly, Finn's bent over his notebook, his pencil clamped in his bright white teeth, deep in thought. I twist further in my seat, angling for a better view of the numbers he's studying, and my hoodie catches on the edge of his binder. He glances up at me, smiling.

Lifting my eyebrows, I try to sound cool as I point at the equations on his paper. "Math homework? No hurricane parties for you?"

He plucks the pencil from his mouth and taps his eraser on the tip of my nose. For the life of me, I can't understand why he's acting like we're friends.

We're not friends.

We haven't been in a very long time.

"Close, Bookworm," he says. The corners of his mischievous green eyes crinkle like he's laughing at me. "I'm calculating wave heights for tonight."

My mouth drops. "What? You can't surf with a hurricane coming."

"I can. I've got it all worked out." He points down at the numbers on his paper.

Ugh. I turn back around. It's none of my business if he wants to kill himself.

"Loosen up, Bookworm. Life's short." His pencil returns to *scritch-scratching* across his paper as I shake my head.

Clamping my teeth shut and willing myself not to respond, I wait for Mr. Richards to continue. My pulse pounds behind my forehead. That boy has a lot of nerve. If I thought for an instant we could ever be friends again, those thoughts died when he told me to *loosen up*. He might be able to loosen up. He might be able to surf in a hurricane. He might not have to take care of anyone or anything but himself.

If anyone—*anyone*—in this school knows how short life is, how quickly things can change, it's me.

CHAPTER FIVE

*Shape your heart to front the hour,
but dream not that the hours will last.*

ALFRED, LORD TENNYSON

After school, I drop Yesenia off at her house, and I can see her parents and siblings already getting ready to evacuate. I envy them—without horses to worry about, they'll be out of here in no time. I hurry home as quickly as I dare, knowing that in the twenty minutes since I pulled out of the parking lot, Mom has texted me probably thirteen times. I don't blame her. She can't help that she's gone from zero to full-out-natural-disaster mode since I said good-bye to her after breakfast, and there's a lot to get done before we can leave.

Taking a steadying breath, I climb the steps to the front door. The sky presses down, heavier than usual, and I realize there's no breeze. It's as if Mother Nature is holding her breath too. I count to ten before opening the screen door and crossing the threshold into the chaos that's our home.

"Oh, Sophie! Thank goodness." Mom pours what's left of the milk into the sink, then tosses the empty container into the recycling tub. "I've hooked up the truck and trailer. Can you start packing Mere's things while I finish cleaning out the fridge?"

"Sure." I glance at Mere, asleep on the sofa with an afghan pulled up to her chin. A *Full House* rerun plays quietly on TV.

The wall above her head that's normally lined with family photos is all but bare. My mother is a force to be reckoned with when she puts her mind to something. And she's totally put her mind to evacuating and protecting and saving what she can.

"I guess we're leaving tonight," I say as she tosses a bag of lettuce into the trash.

"The sooner the better. Aunt Mae's expecting us, and I've called the mainland stable about the horses. Do you have gas?"

"I'm taking my truck?"

"Yes." She adjusts the dial on the weather radio. "I'd rather be in one vehicle, but we can't risk losing your truck. This one's going to be bad."

I know better than to ask where she got her information. The weather service may be predicting a direct hit farther south, they may be predicting a Category 1 storm, but clearly the horses or the seagulls or some other more accurate information source has told my mother otherwise. And for better or for worse, the horses and the gulls are usually right.

"Do you have gas, Sophie?" she asks a second time.

I nod, trying not to think about us traveling in separate vehicles. It's not ideal, but losing the truck to saltwater damage or flooding isn't an option either. "I have over half a tank. And I can find my way to Williamston with my eyes closed."

She pauses to smile at me. "Stop in Manteo and fill up, okay?"

"Okay." The lines will be ridiculously long, but I don't argue.

"Promise," she says, reading my mind.

"I promise."

"We won't try to stick together. It's too stressful—too dangerous. Go at your own pace. By the time we get to Columbia, traffic should be thinning. Let's meet at Dunkin' Donuts, then head to Williamston together." She tosses a bag of chips and a box of graham crackers into the canvas tote bag at her feet for road snacks.

"Now you're speaking my language." I grab the apples she forgot from the basket beside the toaster and drop them into her bag. "The horses can have them while we're pounding down Strawberry Frosteds and Boston Kremes."

Mom takes a moment to smile at me. "I don't know what I'd do without you, sweetheart. I know you'll be careful."

My chest expands a little. Our life has not turned out the way I expected, and I never would have asked for the heartache or the financial stress that came from the accident. But I like that Mom can count on me—that I can alleviate a bit of her anxiety. "Careful's my middle name," I tell her.

Her smile widens as she points to the cat carrier by the front door. "After you pack Mere's stuff, can you put Jim in his crate?"

"Yes, ma'am. On it." I salute and head down the short hall to Mere's room, determined to do everything I can to get us out of here on Mom's schedule. Mere's wardrobe is beyond simple—flannel pajamas, jeans, T-shirts, and hoodies. She gave away all her dance stuff months ago. I have the basics packed—including her toothpaste, toothbrush, and tear-free shampoo—in less than ten minutes. Packing my stuff doesn't take much longer. I pull the three hundred and forty-seven dollars I've been saving for tires from my sock drawer and carefully zip it in the inside pocket, then throw in some extra red pens and highlighters for annotating. A minute later, I carry our bags to the kitchen.

Mom ties a knot in the trash bag as I pass. "While you get Jim, I'll put the trash out and grab my bag. Everything else should be in the truck. Let's try to be on the road before five, okay?"

"What about Mere?" I ask and lift our bags to carry down to the truck.

"Let her rest. I'll wake her when we're ready to walk out." She double-checks the fridge for anything that might spoil as I slip out the door.

The truck and trailer are parked beside the barn, facing out, ready to go. As soon as Mom finishes in the house, we'll load the horses and hit the road. I sling our duffle bags into the backseat of the cab, then quickly survey the bed of the truck. Clear plastic tubs contain extra halters and lead ropes. Bales of hay and a couple of fifty-pound bags of sweet feed and oats hold the buckets and other odds and ends in place. I lift my chin with pride. My friends and teachers think I work hard, but they should see my mom. Sometimes I think she's Wonder Woman.

"Hey, guys! It's me," I call as I turn toward the barn. Jack whinnies. The other horses shuffle around in their stalls. They know something's up, from the change in barometric pressure or the change in my routine or maybe both. And they're restless.

If I'm honest, I have to admit I'm on edge too, so I pick up the pace as I head to the tack room for Jim. "Kitty. Kitty. Jim-bo!" I call. He's not around, so I grab the can of cat treats and shake it. Jim usually doesn't go far. I use the time to inventory the tack room and make sure Mom packed a couple of saddles and bridles and basic first aid supplies. Of course, she has.

Shaking the cat treats again, I step down the center aisle of the barn toward the paddocks and ring out back. When the familiar rumble of Doc Wiggins's diesel truck breaks the quiet, I smile and head back to the parking area in front of the barn. He tips his straw Stetson as the vehicle grinds to a halt. I'm not sure I'd recognize him without the signature hat.

"You evacuating?" I ask as he wrestles the heavy door open and steps down to the driveway.

"After I finish checking on my favorite patients." He winks.

Everyone knows Doc doesn't have favorites. He loves all the animals he cares for . . . and their families too.

"We're all good," I tell him.

"I can see that." He surveys the truck and trailer, then lifts his eyebrows when his gaze settles on the cat treats.

"Just have to find Jim, then we're ready to hit the road."

"Good deal." He nods. "I know you can take care of yourself, and Jim's smart—he'll show up."

I smile, wishing my insides felt more confident than the fake smile on my face. Doc Wiggins is right. I can take care of myself. It's everyone else I'm worried about.

Determined to be efficient and get this show on the road on schedule, I head back through the barn to search for Jim before Doc's truck reaches the end of the driveway.

But there's no sign of Jim anywhere, so I set the treats on the ground and cup my hands around my mouth. Scanning the dunes and horizon behind the barn, I call for Jim and pray for a splotch of orange . . . but find nothing.

When I swallow, my throat feels tight. Jim is a survivor. He's also kind of our family mascot.

He was the first animal I rescued all by myself. The first time I saw him, he was a four-legged kitten on the side of the road. I tried to coax him to the house with food and a soft voice. I left tuna on the front porch, but he had no interest in humans. At that point, he'd rather scavenge than accept handouts, and I knew he'd either take up residence or disappear. Feral cats are funny like that. He finally started sleeping in the barn but kept his distance, always bolting when any of us approached. Then he disappeared for a week or so. The next time we saw him, he was limping—hobbling on three legs. He couldn't move as fast. When I tried to approach, he scuttled off to the scraggly trees at the edge of our property, but not fast enough to hide the bloody stump that had replaced his paw.

I finally caught up with him, and stayed in surgery with the little guy as Doc Wiggins fixed him up. Ever since then, Jim has been part of the family.

The wind picks up, startling me and rustling the seagrass out near the dunes. I grab the cat treats, ready to investigate the gnarled maritime trees behind the manure pile. Movement beside the barn stops me in my tracks.

"Jim?" I call, my voice cracking.

My heart sinks when I see it's a piece of a feed bag blowing in the wind. I glance back at the trees. I don't want Mom to freak if we miss our five o'clock deadline, but there's no way I'm leaving without Jim.

I have to find him.

Now.

CHAPTER SIX

The old order changeth,
yielding place to new.

ALFRED, LORD TENNYSON

After an hour of searching, I'm about to give up. It took a lot of persuading to convince Mom to wait this long for Jim to return. But Jim's lucky. If most cats have nine lives, I'm pretty sure he has nineteen. He survived in the wild as an orphan and is still an excellent mouser despite his missing paw.

But even as I tell myself that, I can't help but worry.

"Sophie, we have to go." My mom sounds upset at the thought of leaving Jim behind, but we're already half an hour past our scheduled departure. I can tell each minute is stressing her out more, and I know we're pushing our luck.

"Where are you, Jim?" I whisper, scanning the area around our house one last time. Nothing.

Finally, Mom fires up the big truck. With no other choice, I walk toward my own truck, trying to convince myself Jim will be all right. And then, just as I'm about to climb into the driver's seat, I see a flash of orange.

"You smart boy!" I croon as I pick up Jim and hug him tight.

Of course he would have perfect timing—just like Doc said. Instead of roughing it out in a hurricane, he shows up just in time to take a mini vacation to Aunt Mae's, where he'll be spoiled with lots and lots of salmon and tuna treats.

With a few more compliments, I place him in the crate on the backseat of Mom's truck. He circles a few times, curls up in a ball, and closes his eyes like he doesn't have a care in the world. I smile at his whiskered face as I close the truck door. Mom blows me a quick kiss. The diesel engine groans as she changes gears and eases forward down the sandy driveway and toward the main road.

I just need to grab my backpack. Then I can focus on the road and Strawberry Frosteds and Boston Kremes, and maybe if we're feeling really adventurous, a couple of Butter Pecan Macchiatos. I find my pack right where I left it on the floor beside the front door. As I hoist it onto my shoulder, a large black trash bag in the kitchen catches my eye. Cleaning out the fridge is kind of a waste if you leave the food to spoil.

I grab the bag, wondering how Mom could have walked past the trash and forgotten it. That's not like her at all. Clearly, she's beyond stressed. For the thousandth time, I wish Mom had a reliable partner—a spouse who didn't bolt when life got too hard. I'm pulling the back door closed behind me when the bottom of the trash bag falls out. My stomach twists at the mound of cottage cheese mixed with leftover taco meat and a couple of other unidentifiable mystery foods.

Great.

I shoot Mom a text, letting her know I'll be a little bit

behind because of the mess. It takes a good ten minutes to re-bag the trash and pour a cup of water over the icky residue on the deck. By the time I finally toss the bag in the back of the truck and hit the road, I feel like Mom and Mere are hours away. I tell myself I'm being silly and focus on navigating the already deserted roads. The safety-conscious residents, like Mom, packed up and left immediately. The less cautious will leave in one final rush. And by this time of the year, the tourists are gone. That leaves the road all to me. As I drive, I try to avoid looking at the angry white caps of the Atlantic churning out past the dunes or listening to the doom-and-gloom radio announcer narrating the progress of the storm. Lost in my thoughts of Mom and Mere, I don't see the boards in the road until it's almost too late. Gripping the steering wheel, I grit my teeth and swerve to avoid the wood. Who knows how many nails the stuff is riddled with. My right front tire clicks when I clip the edge of one board. Thankfully, I manage to avoid swerving off the road or running over the boards head-on.

My hands unclench a little when the radio switches back to its regular programming—some sappy love song. I relax but keep my eyes peeled for more debris in the road.

Then the truck jerks. A *thwump-thwump* ignites a new spark of fear in my gut. Clicking off the radio, I ease my foot from the accelerator and lean forward, listening. My heart sinks when I recognize the sound.

I've blown one of my bald tires. I should have told Mom they were in bad shape, even though I know it wouldn't have helped. She doesn't have four hundred dollars lying around to buy tires. Plus, I was so very, very close. Between the discount the tire guy promised me and the three hundred and forty-seven bucks now zipped in the duffle in Mom's truck, I was only seventy-three dollars from a new set of tires.

I look around on the road for another car that could help, but I'm totally alone, and the screech of metal scraping pavement can't be good. I'm about to cause more than tire damage to Dad's old truck, so I pull off the side of the road. Tapping my forehead on the steering wheel, I pray for a miracle, or better yet, a way to turn back time. When I step out of the truck, the temperature has dropped several degrees. The wind rakes at my hair, and I shiver as I go to check the damage.

My front tire is gone, shredded and left in a trail on the road behind me. The rim, or whatever it's called, has sunk several inches into the sand on the side of the road. Dad taught me how to change a tire a million years ago, but I'm not so sure I remember how to do it on my own. And I'm definitely sure I don't want to be caught trying to wrestle a spare tire onto my ancient truck during a hurricane.

As I survey my surroundings, the rumble of a large engine growls over the moaning wind. Maybe it's an answer to my prayers in the form of a police officer or one of those giant trucks that hauls cars on the highway. I squint down the road. As the approaching vehicle comes into focus, my stomach feels like it dropped to my knees. Holding my breath, I grip the tail of my OBX T-shirt in my fists.

I'd recognize that vomit-green, rusted-out deathtrap anywhere. The surfboards and rack on top are probably worth more than the actual car. Before I have time to formulate a plan or run screaming over the dunes, the vehicle screeches to a stop beside me, and out pops my rescuer. No Prince Charmings or white knights for this girl—I get Finn Sanders.

As he's all I've got at this point, I squinch my face into what's supposed to be a smile.

"What's up, Bookworm?" He screws the cap back on a bottle of Dr Pepper and sets it on the hood of his car.

Heat prickles my chest as I bite my tongue.

"Changing a flat not on the syllabus?" He cocks one eyebrow and flashes the smile that earned him extensions on incomplete homework assignments in eighth grade.

"I'm sure I can figure it out." I lift my chin, not wanting to ask him for help.

His face goes serious, but I'm pretty sure a smile still tugs at the corner of his mouth. "I don't mind changing a flat. I'm good with my hands." One of his eyebrows lifts mischievously.

"Thanks." I ignore his attempt at humor. Sea oats rustle and swish as a rush of wind flattens them to the sand out on the dunes. I want to argue. I could totally change a tire if I had time to figure it out, but time is the one thing I don't have much of today.

"So where's the spare?" He shoves his hands into his front pockets. Something about the tilt of his head and the quirk of his mouth says he's testing me. And if there's one thing I don't like, it's failing tests. You don't earn a perfect score on the pre-SAT if you can't think fast and use the process of elimination. I point to the back of the truck. "It's under the bed."

He props himself against the side of the truck like we have all day. "Where's the jack?"

Crap. I have no idea, and it could be anywhere. I open my mouth but can't think of anything to say.

Smirking, he heads around the front of the truck. "It's behind the passenger seat."

I could live without the attitude, but in all fairness, I wasn't exactly a ball of sunshine when he approached me at school this morning. At least he seems to know what he's doing. He extracts a plastic box with several crowbar-looking tools and what I assume is the jack, then carries them to the back of the truck, where he lays them on the edge of the road. When he shimmies under the truck on his back, his T-shirt rises, revealing a sliver of his toned abs. Thank God he can't see my face or see me staring in the general vicinity of his waistband. His ego is big enough already. I'd light my hair on fire before I'd give him the satisfaction of thinking I was checking him out.

"Uh . . . Einstein . . ."

My body stiffens at the way he says *Einstein*—half confused, half concerned. "Yes?"

"I hate to break the bad news, but your spare's gone."

"What do you mean *gone*? That can't be."

"You want to look for yourself?"

"Yes. Yes, I do, actually." Squatting, I twist my neck, trying to glimpse the underneath of the truck. It's pointless, though. He has no reason to lie, and from what I can see, there isn't a spare.

He slides out from under the truck, stands next to me, and slaps me on the back. "Guess you're stuck with me, Bookworm."

My shoulders tense. My legs tense. I think maybe my toenails tense. I don't want to be alone with Finn, even if it's to flee to safety in the face of a storm.

But on the other hand, I'm not about to wait for someone else to come along and help me. "Could you take me to the forest ranger station in Manteo? I have friends there."

Well, Mom has a friend there—Carla, who's one of the

rangers. She's about the only person I can think of who would still be around and willing to give me a ride to Williamston with an evacuation in progress and a hurricane bearing down. By now, Yesenia and her family will be across the bridge, and there's no way I can ask Mom to turn around and get me.

"Sure." He steps toward his Blazer, opening the passenger door for me.

I turn back to the truck to grab my belongings, leaving the bag of trash where it is. As I reach into the backseat, I spot Mere's compass—one of the few trinkets she still cares about—and grab it too. Finn raises an eyebrow at the device.

"It's my sister's." I don't explain how Dad bought each of us our own compass before our last big family vacation to Yellowstone, or why Mere still keeps hers around. Thankfully, he doesn't ask.

"I just have to run supplies up to a relative in Corolla first," he says.

"You do know high tide is coming. Right? And that Collington Road washes out on a windy day. Parts of the beach road could wash out long before a storm hits."

"I don't have a choice. My uncle's going to ride it out. He needs fuel, batteries, water." He points to supplies piled in the backseat beside a massive plastic tub overflowing with what appears to be several wetsuits.

I want to argue, to ask him what kind of stupid relative would *ride out* a mandatory evacuation, but I keep my mouth shut. It's his car, and he's the only person to come along since I pulled over.

As much as I hate to admit it, I'm no longer the one in control.

CHAPTER SEVEN

We cannot be kind to each other here for even an hour.

ALFRED, LORD TENNYSON

We ride north in silence. I send a quick text to Carla, who says she can get me to Williamston. Then I draft a longer one to Mom, telling her about the flat, not to worry, and that Carla's taking me to her. But now my dumb phone refuses to cooperate. The delivery receipt won't load.

Come on. Come on. I hold my breath. This message has to go through or Mom will freak. I exhale when it finally sends. But the farther north we drive, the more my service bars dwindle. Signals are always a bit spotty up here but not this bad. The approaching storm must already be taking its toll. I feel like I'm letting go of a lifeline to my family, at least until we head south to Manteo.

I sit still, staring out the passenger window and trying not to touch any of Finn's stuff. The inside of his car isn't exactly dirty, but it definitely falls on the sloppy side of the cleanliness spectrum. Think several beef jerky wrappers, a couple empty Dr Pepper bottles, and at least one empty Doritos bag, not to mention surfing magazines and what looks like some kind of textbook on homeopathic healing.

The boy's an oxymoron. What kind of person eats this much junk, drinks this much high-fructose corn syrup, and owns a book on natural remedies? I shift sideways, trying to get comfortable in the cramped space. But my foot brushes an empty donut box, causing a tattered book to slide to the floor. At least I think it's a book. The thing is more duct tape than actual cardboard and paper. Clearly, it's been read about eighty-bazillion times. I lift it to read the title—*Don't Sweat the Small Stuff . . . and It's All Small Stuff*. It's heavy from all the tape and looks like it would hold meaty information despite the silly title.

"Uh, sorry," I say, apologizing when I realize Finn looks uncomfortable with me handling his raggedy book. Studying the minefield of crackling papers and plastic bottles surrounding my feet, I bend over to return the book to its special place atop the donut box.

"No. I'm sorry. I really need to clean my car," he says, looking relieved when I return the book to its rightful place.

"You weren't expecting a passenger." I can tell he's trying to be nice, and he did help me. My foot rustles an unidentifiable bag. We make eye contact, and I smile, a little peace offering. "But maybe you should cut back a bit on the junk food."

"A guy's gotta eat." He shrugs and turns back to the road.

I should keep my mouth shut. Of course, I don't. "That's not actually food, you know? It'll kill you," I say, pointing at a beef jerky wrapper.

"But it tastes so good. I'll die happy." He rubs his stomach area.

I shoot a fleeting look at the big white textbook with the

herbs and vegetables on the cover. He follows my gaze, then turns back to the road. His knuckles whiten a shade, like he's uncomfortable again. I don't understand why this boy, who doesn't seem concerned about an oncoming hurricane, gets all nervous when I draw attention to his books, which can't be all that important if they live in the landfill that is his vehicle.

"Hey, it's protein," he says, reverting to his class-clown demeanor. When a gust of wind threatens to blow us off the road, he appears completely unfazed.

Humph. I cross my arms, telling myself to bite my tongue. I'm not the healthiest person on the face of the planet, but calling beef jerky protein is a bit generous. "It's sort of protein. In an artificial-chemical-mystery-meat kind of way."

"Are you a dietician or something?"

"No, just trying to help. Speaking of which, we should really be heading south while we still can. Have you listened to the news?" Somehow, he manages to bring out the snippy verbal side of me that normally spends most of its time in hibernation. Unless it involves a class participation grade, I'm generally pretty good at keeping my mouth shut and my sarcastic comments inside my head.

"I don't listen to the news. Way too bad for my health."

I twist to look at him, ready to crack a joke of my own, but his face is . . . serious? I catch a glimpse of my open mouth in the rearview mirror. *Way too bad for his health?* Is he kidding? Is he crazy? I can't even formulate words.

As we near the end of the paved road north of the last lighthouse, I close my eyes to the count of three, breathe deeply, and try a new tactic. "Maybe we could listen to the radio for a minute. You know? Just in case."

He reaches for a knob on the old radio. "Sure. But it won't change anything. I have to get this stuff to Zeke."

I don't respond. I strain to hear what the radio guy says between bursts of crackling static.

". . . Repeat: the Emergency Management System has moved the mandatory evacuation to eleven o'clock tonight. Hurricane Harry is now a Category 2 storm. Based on the currently increasing wind speeds, it has the potential to reach Category 3 by the time it makes landfall. The forecast now predicts the storm will hit the Northern Outer Banks near high tide, creating an unpredictable storm surge. Please take all precautions to evacuate tonight. Expected road outages will prevent emergency personnel from reaching residents after that time."

I have to stifle a gasp and clench the armrest tightly at the thought of a storm that bad. But paradox-boy seems completely unworried as he continues in the opposite direction of safety.

He taps out a happy rhythm on the steering wheel with his thumbs as if he didn't just hear the same warning I did. Chewing my lower lip and sitting on my hands, I search for a more persuasive argument than the weather forecast we just heard. But I come up blank.

"What time is it?" I ask, nodding at the cracked leather watchband circling his wrist. Maybe drawing his attention to the passing hours will spark some sense of urgency.

He shrugs without checking his watch.

"Um, I'm pretty sure the thing on your wrist will tell you."

"Oh, this?" He glances down and jiggles his watch.

"Yeah, that." I try not to sound sarcastic. I really do.

"It hasn't worked in months."

I don't want to ask. I know the answer will be something ridiculous, but I can't help myself. The boy's an enigma begging to be solved. "Then why are you wearing it?"

"It's symbolic." He continues his sporadic drum solo on the steering wheel.

I press my lips together.

Don't ask, Sophie.

Don't ask.

"Of what?" *Crap.*

"Of time." He glances over at me, like I'm purposely being stupid. When I don't say anything, he continues. "It really does fly, you know? I want to make sure I get the most out of it. Plus, it's still correct twice a day."

I have no response to that, so I check my phone despite its dwindling battery power and see it's almost seven o'clock. We continue in silence until we reach the ramp to the four-wheel-drive beach road, where Finn pulls over to let air out of his tires. At least he has some knowledge of where and how to drive on the beach. But his experience with the upper reaches of the four-wheel-drive area isn't helping the nerves simmering in my belly.

It's not just the storm now. I haven't been north of the sound-to-sea fence Mom and Dad fought so hard to build since before Dad left. It's the best thing I remember them doing together before the accident ruined our lives—before he walked out on us.

Finn glances at me when we reach the packed sand near the shoreline. "You okay, Bookworm? You look carsick."

"I'm fine." I'd rather swallow mouthfuls of sand than disclose to Finn Sanders all my family drama.

"Whoa." He points at the dune line to our left. Several wild horses huddle together near a line of weathered utility poles. Heavy-duty wire cable links the poles one to the other, forming an almost indestructible fence. The gray poles resemble weary soldiers, marching inland as far as the eye can see and out into the choppy Atlantic in the opposite direction.

The horses could be statues in iron, copper, and marble except for their long manes and tails gliding on the northerly wind. They look like Jack and Roxie and Dolly with a few glaring exceptions. They're more compact than the typical domesticated horse. Their backs are shorter, making them more square and less rectangular. And if you look closely, their tails are set lower on their hindquarters, evidence of their Spanish Mustang heritage.

Finn eases his foot off the brake as he studies the horses. "I haven't seen them this far south since . . . I don't think I've seen them this close to the fence since they were penned in."

My heart constricts. I'm not sure if it's a wave of grief or the way his voice drops on the word *penned* as though it disgusts him. Probably, it's a combination of the two.

"They're not penned in. That fence saves their lives from . . ." I want to say *reckless drivers like you*. Instead I grip the door handle as we bounce over an uneven patch of sand.

"That fence is a cage—keeping them from expanding their habitat. They're no better off than if they were in a zoo." He shrugs like he doesn't care enough to argue, but I'm pretty sure the arch of his eyebrow confirms my gut instinct—he's challenging me, like he thinks he scored a point in this debate that's not really a debate.

I level my eyes on his profile, trying to sound confident and casual at the same time. "They have seventy-five-hundred acres to roam. My parents organized the fundraising and building of that fence. They love those horses. They'd be extinct if it weren't for people like my parents. Even with the fence, they're critically endangered."

For once, he shuts up.

I scan the beach for more horses, determined to keep my mouth closed, but I can't. "My mom says the horses migrate ahead of the storms. They've moved the evacuation up ten hours. Surely if your friend Zeke or whatever his name is—"

"He's my uncle."

"If your *uncle* lives up here year-round, he must know the risks. He must be prepared in case of emergency, especially if he plans to stay put. If you won't turn back, will you at least hurry? Please."

Mom's the superstitious one. Not me. Logically, I don't think the horses can predict weather that far off. Maybe they sense the dropping barometric pressure or something, but they can't possibly know where the storm will make landfall when the weather service isn't even certain. But Mom's been right so often when it comes to the weather and her animals, I can't help but consider the possibility she might be right again. The horses might be pushed up against their southern boundary in an attempt to dodge the oncoming storm.

"Relax, Worrywart. We've got hours—more than enough time to get you to Manteo and a dependable ride." His biceps twitch beneath his short sleeves when he jerks left to avoid a wave rushing in farther than the previous ones.

Refusing to be baited, I clamp down on my lower lip with my teeth and contemplate the absence of sea birds. I pray they're floating to safety on the winds ahead of the storm or that their automatically clenching toe muscles will keep them safely perched in a sturdy tree somewhere. I try not to think about Doc Wiggins telling me about the birds that seek refuge in the eye of the hurricane, then die of fatigue or starvation if the storm outlasts their stamina.

Marker signs count off every quarter mile as we head farther north. We've traveled several miles when Finn veers left and stomps the gas pedal. He thrusts us over the dune line and into a grove of gnarled trees, heading for a shack that blends in with the maritime forest around it.

"How did you know where to turn?" I ask, marveling at his sense of direction. We passed the last vacation rental a ways back. Since then it's been nothing but a stretch of dunes and sea oats that all look pretty much alike.

He lifts his shoulders, like he's never thought about it before. "Instinct, I guess."

At the sound of Finn's Blazer, a hunched figure barely visible from behind bushy eyebrows and a chest-length beard opens the door and tosses up a hand in greeting. When his eyes land on me in the passenger seat, his hand drops. It's hard to say because of all the hair, but I'm pretty sure his leathery face tightens.

Mine feels kind of stiff as well. I don't know what I expected from Finn's uncle; maybe an older version of Finn with deeper creases at the corners of the eyes. But this guy's more *Duck Dynasty* than surfer dude. I've seen my fair share of salty, commercial fishermen, and a number of hardcore mountain men when we visited Mom's relatives in West Virginia, but I've never seen anyone like this guy on the Outer Banks. I try not to stare as Zeke approaches the Blazer.

Finn jumps down to the sand. They move to the back of the car and open the door.

I turn and smile. "Hi," I say.

Finn sort of smiles. But I think he's trying not to smile more than he's actually smiling, like he's in on a joke I missed. He hands Zeke several huge packs of batteries, gallons of water, and two cardboard boxes. Zeke stacks the supplies on the ground.

"Who's that?" Zeke asks in a gruff voice without acknowledging me.

"A friend from school. Her name's Sophie."

I don't know which shocks me more, Zeke's bad manners or Finn Sanders introducing me as a friend. Clearly, his definition of *friend* and mine vary.

"Too bad you won't be able to grab a quick set of waves. They've gone off the Richter in the last hour or two." Zeke turns to lift one of the boxes stacked on the sand.

Finn's voice drops. "Like how off the Richter?" He glances over his shoulder, like he's looking to see if I'm listening.

Not only am I listening, but alarm bells sound in my brain. I know enough about Finn to realize tempting him with waves *off the Richter* is like asking a stressed-out chocoholic if he wants a Hershey's bar.

I open my mouth to speak, but Finn beats me to it. "Sophie, you want to see something awesome?"

"Uh . . . *no*. I want to get off this island."

"Sorry, bro." Zeke slaps Finn on the back, then starts carting his goods inside. "I'm going out there before the waves get too serious."

Finn's the one who looks sick now, like someone set him

up on the world's most awkward blind date. He drags a hand through his shaggy hair when he speaks. "This is a once-in-a-lifetime opportunity, Bookworm. Can you give me like twenty minutes?"

"Twenty minutes to kill yourself? Sure. Have fun."

He ignores my sarcasm and snatches a wet suit from the tub in the backseat. Leaning over the top of the car, he unfastens hooks and latches on the board rack as he speaks. "You're the best. Make yourself comfortable."

"I was kidding!" I tell him.

I want to bang my head on the dashboard. I want to lecture him on the dangerous surf conditions. I want to close my eyes, wave a magic wand, and transport myself from this rattrap of a vehicle to the cab of Mom's truck. But there's no use arguing with him. I can tell he's going to do what he wants to do when he wants to do it.

I try to strike a bargain. "What if you're not back in twenty minutes?"

"I will be."

"If you're not, I'm leaving."

"Fine." He steps down from the running board, pulling a white surfboard off the roof and resting it on his shoulder.

I level my eyes on his face to make sure he knows I'm serious. "I'm leaving in your car."

He slings the wet suit over his other shoulder, hesitating for a second before responding. "We don't have to worry about that because I'll be back in twenty."

As I watch him jog off, I decide I'm fairly sure he's lying.

CHAPTER EIGHT

When you meet triumph or disaster, treat these imposters alike.

ALFRED, LORD TENNYSON

Eighteen minutes later, I've flipped through two surfing magazines and the book on natural eating and healing. The sections pertaining to digestion are heavily highlighted with notes scribbled in the margins. No wonder. The boy's a walking gut bomb waiting to explode. I'm pretty sure he could skip the research, eat real food, and eliminate whatever's upsetting his system.

After nineteen minutes, I glance over the dunes with mixed emotions—half hoping Finn will come waltzing back with a goofy smile, a wisecrack, and the desire to chauffeur me to Manteo ASAP—half hoping he won't show so I can hit the road by myself.

At twenty minutes, I crawl into the driver's seat. I've never driven a stick shift, but it can't be that difficult. Yesenia's mom has a stick shift, and she explained how the clutch works. We just never got around to practicing, since Yesenia hasn't bothered to get her driver's license. Between her siblings and me being able to drive her around, she says there's no need.

My feet barely reach the pedals, so I scoot to the edge of the seat and turn the key in the ignition. The engine doesn't fire up or even sputter. Something near the keyhole *click, click, clicks.* That's about it. I try a second time. And a third. Nothing.

Finn's car looks like it's survived World War III, but it drove fine for him. I must be doing something wrong. I suck down a deep breath, trying to calm my racing heart and think clearly. This would be a great time to pull up a tutorial video online, but my service is still hovering at zero bars. I'm anxious enough without thinking about my phone and all the alerts and planner alarms I'm missing, so I try to focus on driving.

For the life of me, I don't know what I'm doing wrong. The car is in gear. I'm turning the key. It must have something to do with the clutch. I figure I can't hurt this beast of a vehicle, so I press the clutch to the floor and give it another try. The green ogre rumbles to life. With the clutch still mashed to the floor, I move the gearshift down to reverse and give it some gas. Ha! I'm not breaking any speed barriers, but I'm moving—that is until I attempt to stop, turn, and shift to first. The fickle monster sputters and dies.

I manage to restart the engine but stall out a second time before I close the gap between Zeke's shack and the dunes. It's no use. Driving this contraption solo is almost as dumb as surfing in the face of an oncoming hurricane, and I prefer not to do stupid. Defeated, I crawl back to the passenger seat to fume and curse the universe.

I don't want to give Finn the satisfaction of chasing after him, so I search the floorboard for something more interesting to read than surfing magazines or homeopathic textbooks. I accidentally knock the duct-taped book with the silly title off its spot on the donut box, and the reinforced cover falls open. The pages are dog-eared and highlighted all over the place. Annotations cover every speck of white space in the margins. Mr. Richards would be impressed. I'm pretty sure in middle school, Finn paid less-than-stellar attention to detail when reading and taking notes, but high school Finn is certainly invested in not sweating the small stuff.

Despite my curiosity, it seems like an invasion of privacy to mess with such a well-loved book, so I close it, returning it to its place of honor atop the Krispy Kreme shrine. Then I stare out the side window and draft a mental T-chart, weighing the pros and cons of going to get Finn versus waiting on him to return.

Pros: I want to get out of here. Now. For me, for Mom, for Mere, for Jim . . . for my general safety. For Finn's safety too, however little he seems to care about it.

The cons side of the T-chart remains empty. As I search for a reason to wait on Finn's return, besides my pride and the fact the sky has turned charcoal gray, I twist the key in the ignition to turn on the radio.

It crackles to life in the middle of another hurricane announcement. ". . . water is inches from Highway 12 in Hatteras. Dare County Emergency Management has started door-to-door inquiries to ensure residents have evacuated. Several factors have combined to create especially dangerous conditions. Repeat: please evacuate now."

Enough is enough. I flick the radio off in the middle of the man's dramatic pause, jump down to the sand, and storm toward the dunes. Movement in the tangled trees beside Zeke's shack catches my eye. I freeze, zeroing in on a chestnut horse hunkered down in the knotted stand of spindly trunks that camouflage him. The poor thing couldn't have picked a worse time to lose his herd. Wherever they are, they seem to have left him to fend for himself.

I turn away, unable to look at him once I realize just how much I feel like that lonely horse. Dull pressure squeezes my heart. As I tromp toward the ocean, I recite facts I learned from Dad about the horses he fought to protect. Humans generally do more harm than good when they interfere. A horse died a few years ago after tourists fed it apples and carrots and other treats its system couldn't handle. The fact I repeat again and again is how the horses have survived here for over five hundred years. They were left behind by Spanish explorers who couldn't scrape out a life. Humans wouldn't thrive here for several hundred years, but the horses did just fine under the harshest conditions.

The horse will be fine. And I will be too.

Breathless, I crest the mountain of sand and spot a pair of jeans, flip-flops, and a T-shirt piled on the ground. The beach is empty. But still, I would never just strip down to my underwear on the wide-open beach. Obviously, Finn has zero issues with that.

I glance out to sea and spy two white boards bobbing in the angry surf. Waving a hand above my head, I try to get Finn or Zeke's attention. Apparently, they're hyper-focused on staying afloat in the churning water and dimming light. As I watch, Finn angles his board toward the beach. His broad shoulders and strong strokes look determined. He rises with a forming wave. In one fluid movement, he pushes himself to standing. Turning parallel to the beach, he glides in front of the racing funnel of white until it consumes him and the back of the board. Air catches in my throat. There's no way he can escape the water surrounding him on all sides.

But he does.

Somehow, he shoots out a tiny opening in the funnel and races ahead of the collapsing wall of water. He shouts a cry of victory over the crashing waves. I watch, speechless. It's beautiful in a kind of terrifying way.

I shake off the trance. There is no way—*no way*—I'm going to be sucked in by his cool wetsuit or daring stunts. I wave both hands over my head, jumping up and down for added emphasis. By some miracle, he turns his head in my direction. When he does, the tail end of the wave he just outran charges in and capsizes him.

Holding my breath, I clamp my hand over my mouth. He's gone. I know what it's like to be knocked off a boogie board and dragged under on a typical summer day—to tumble and scrape against a carpet of crushed shells, to want to reach for the surface when you have no idea which direction is up or down. And today is anything but typical.

I run toward the water as Zeke paddles toward shore. Apparently he has eyes in the back of his head or something and saw the whole thing. "Finn!" he shouts.

A board rockets from the water fifty yards down the beach. There's no cocky surfer attached to it. I sprint toward it, but the loose sand makes speed difficult.

No. No. No. This can't be happening. I told him it was stupid. "Finn! Finn!" I scream as though he's going to hear me under the turbulent water.

The boy's arrogant and annoying and impulsive, and I told him this was idiotic. But I would never, never wish anything bad on him. And now it's my fault, my fault he's—I don't dare think the words.

"Dear God, please, please—" I'll pray, beg, whatever it takes to bring Finn to the surface. I couldn't live with myself or the guilt if he died. I should've been more emphatic about not surfing.

But I wasn't.

And now Finn is gone.

CHAPTER NINE

*Let the great world spin for ever down
the ringing grooves of change.*

ALFRED, LORD TENNYSON

There!" Zeke yells as he charges up the beach toward me.

I squint in the general direction of his pointed finger, but I don't see anything. Then the surf retreats, leaving behind a life-size lump of black. I take off. My calves scream in protest against the sand pulling at my feet. Zeke catches up to me seconds later. Without words, we each grab an arm and drag a limp Finn to safety.

Zeke rolls Finn onto his back for a better look.

He's not dead—not even unconscious. The idiot is laughing. *Laughing.*

"That was . . . awesome." He pushes himself up on an elbow.

My pulse pounds in my throat. I fight the urge to draw back and kick him in the ribs. Glaring down at him with my best death stare, I cross my arms over my chest. "You scared me, idiot."

One corner of his mouth turns up. "Aww, see, I knew you cared, Bookworm."

I almost growl. "You . . . you . . . jerk. You scared the crap out of me."

"*Jerk?* That's the best you've got . . ." His voice trails off as he wipes salt water from his face with the back of his hand.

Refusing to be baited into another ridiculous argument, I swipe at the tangled hair whipping around my face. "How can you even joke at a time like this? I thought you were dead."

The wind whips at the ocean frothing behind him. These are not your typical Outer Banks waves with their dependable and evenly timed crest-trough-crest rhythm. These waves are higher, harder breaking, and hungrier. They almost made a meal of Finn.

Dad once told me three things must work together to create waves like this—a hurricane force trifecta of speed, distance, and duration. Then I remember what one of the radio announcers said about the Category 2 storm and the timing of the high tide, and the sense of urgency I've been fighting to keep under wraps suddenly threatens to overflow.

Zeke offers Finn his hand. He takes it and lets himself be pulled to standing. "Not dead but close," Finn says. "I bet mouth-to-mouth would speed the recovery."

My jaw clicks when it falls open. "Not in this lifetime. By the way, Highway 12 is almost under water in Hatteras. We might want to get this show on the road unless we plan to ride it out here."

Zeke gives Finn a little shove toward the dunes. The man seems a thousand times more frightened by the thought of overnight, female company than he does by Finn's stupid stunt or the threat of an oncoming hurricane.

Ch-ching.

Score two for me.

In another lifetime, I might be curious about Zeke and his loner life out on the beach. In this lifetime, all I care about is getting to Mom. If she doesn't hear from me soon, she'll freak, and she can't afford to be distracted while pulling a heavy load and looking out for Mere.

"Hey, what about my board?" Finn asks.

"Dude, that thing's history," Zeke says as they follow me toward the dunes, and Finn looks sadder than I've ever seen him.

No one speaks till we reach the shack. Neither of them comments on the fact that the Blazer's parked in an entirely different spot or that the clouds are getting darker and we're losing sunlight.

"You sure you don't want to go with us?" Finn takes his sandy clothes from Zeke and steps around to the driver's side of the car. I study the ground, as there's absolutely no telling what the boy does or does not wear under his wetsuit. And I'm not taking any chances.

"Yes," Zeke says.

When I chance a quick look up, he's glancing toward the dark patch of trees behind the shack where I saw the horse.

"I have stuff to do here," he says. "I'll head to the lighthouse if things get bad. If the lighthouse goes, the island goes. If the island goes, I may as well go with her."

That's cheerful, I think. I chew on my bottom lip, glancing through the windows of the Blazer. As Finn wiggles into his shirt, I pull open the passenger-side door and slide in.

Finn tightens his belt as he walks toward Zeke and pulls him in for that shoulder-bump, back-slap thing guys call a hug. "Be safe," he says.

"Always, man." Zeke heads to the shack as if it's just another day in the life of an Outer Banks hermit.

Finn steps up onto the running board, then slides into the driver's seat and throws the Blazer in reverse. My head jerks backward, but I don't complain. I'm thrilled to finally be on the road, heading toward the mainland, heading toward safety, heading toward Mom.

We drive in silence. My practical backpack and duffel rest on the backseat right beside his water sports equipment and a Kit Kat wrapper. The wind blows harder now, and Finn has to drive much closer to the dunes on the ride south. I see no signs of the horses now—or any other wildlife. They've surely holed up somewhere away from the gale and the rising tide.

When we reach the paved road in Corolla, I almost start to relax, at least until Finn opens his big fat mouth.

"Since you're in a hurry, we can take a shortcut," he suggests, pointing toward a narrow street on our left.

The beach road here is paved and nothing like the four-wheel-drive beach road behind us, but it is the only main road this far north. During the summer, it's bumper to bumper almost every day. But this is October. There's nobody here and no reason to risk a downed power line or twists or turns or anything else on tight neighborhood streets, even if they shorten the distance some.

"No. Let's take the main road. It's safer."

"What's so great about *safety*? The best things in life aren't safe—surfing, hang gliding. Even driving a car isn't safe, is it?" He gives the steering wheel a quick turn, causing the front end to cross the yellow line as he whips us down a side street.

"You're . . . you're . . ." I grab the door handle. Words

that would traumatize Mom ricochet in my head, but I don't say them.

"Spit it out. Let it loose." He seems amused by my stuttering.

If this were a movie, I'd demand he stop the car, smack the smirk off his face, and then go storming off on my own into the hurricane. But I'm not in a movie, and I'm not that impulsive. I release my death grip on the door handle and ball my hands into fists in my lap. "You're a jerk, Finn Sanders." I spit the words in his general direction without meeting his eyes, realizing I've used the same insult twice now.

Laughing, he smacks the steering wheel. "You're funny, Sophie March."

Refusing to look at him, I study the road ahead, steadying myself when we feel another blast of wind. Honestly, I didn't know he remembered my last name. But clearly, he doesn't remember me that well, because I don't have a funny bone in my body—sarcastic, maybe. On a really good day, maybe even witty. Funny—not so much.

Before I can remind him that he doesn't know anything about me anymore, that we're not friends, that he stood me up for my first and only high school dance, something smashes into the windshield. He jerks the wheel, and the next thing I know we're lurching off the side of the road. He overcorrects, yanking us back onto the smooth asphalt. But the back of the Blazer fishtails, whipping back and forth. Somehow, we remain on the road. Time slows, magnifying the crash of glass and the squeal of brakes.

Some sort of self-defense mechanism must kick in, because I watch the action unfold in front of me like something happening to someone on TV. Bracing my hands on the dashboard, I calmly accept the inevitably of what's to come. Part of me wonders how Mom and Mere will make it without me. Part of me accepts the unavoidable. The ringing in my ears helps to mute the screech of metal on pavement.

A distant scream that might be Finn's hangs in the air. The last thing I see before a neck-jerking impact is the line of mailboxes and stand of dark pine trees barreling toward us.

CHAPTER TEN

*To strive, to seek, to find,
and not to yield.*

ALFRED, LORD TENNYSON

When something cold and wet smacks my cheek, I open my eyes. Blinking, I try to clear the fogginess clouding my thoughts. It's more dark than light outside. Icy drops of water prick my face through the missing glass in the windshield before me. I glance to my left at the shadowy figure slumped over his deflated airbag and steering wheel, and a wave of memories crashes over me. Oh, God. We are in deep, deep trouble.

I have no idea how much time has passed. It's probably only been a few minutes since the accident—otherwise it would be pitch dark by now. We're on the back end of twilight and speeding toward real-deal darkness, but there's still a bit of gray in the sky. However long it's been, it was long enough for the wind to increase from a whistle to a roar. The person hanging forward against his seat belt is Finn, and he's not cracking any jokes about mouth-to-mouth this time.

I push the airbag out of my lap and claw at my own seat

belt, desperate to escape. The picture of my family's crumpled car in the newspaper flashes behind my eyelids. I realize I could've died just now and left Mom with yet another tragedy.

A gust of wind rocks the car, distracting me from the panic gripping my heart and chest. When I squint into the murky shadows, the pine trees above us bend at precarious angles. Somewhere in the distance, a sharp crack of what sounds like splintering wood snaps above the droning wind.

I reach over to wiggle Finn's elbow. "Finn. Wake up. We've got to get out of here."

When I squeeze his shoulder, a groan escapes his pale lips. His head lolls to the side, eyelids fluttering a bit but not opening. I shiver as cold wind nibbles at the exposed skin on my face and neck. We need to hole up somewhere safe. Waiting for help is not an option, and anywhere would be better than a wrecked car beneath a stand of shallow-rooted pine trees.

Last I remember, we were racing down a residential side street. Then what must have been a massive tree branch hit us out of nowhere. The mailbox on the hood of the car means there must be at least one house beyond the trees and sandy hills to our left. I just have to find it in the dark. No, not *me*. *We* have to find it. Finn's not my favorite person, but I'm not leaving him out here to fend for himself. Plus, he doesn't look like he'll be able to fend for himself anytime soon.

I unbuckle my seat belt, prepared to do whatever I need to do to keep us both safe. He's in good shape. I didn't see an ounce of fat on him when he was dressing back at Zeke's—not that I was looking. Yet he's really tall and has to outweigh me by a lot. We're not going anywhere till he can walk.

"Finn, please. Wake up." I gently lift and tilt his head back against the headrest, thankful when his chest rises and falls. But he doesn't respond. My fingers graze a massive bump near his temple. It's too dark to tell how badly he's hit his head, but I start to worry about a concussion. When I unbuckle him, he slides to the left against the door. His head touches the glass. He winces, his eyes opening to slits. I wave my hand in front of his face. "Finn. Finn. It's Sophie."

His eyelids flutter again, threatening to close.

I lean in so close his shallow breath brushes my cheeks. "Finn, stay with me, please. Look at me. We've got to get out of here."

His lips part, but no sound comes out. The trees beside the car crackle and pop under the force of the wind. Finn's Adam's apple slides down his neck, and his eyes widen. He manages a wobbly nod, but even that seems to require tremendous effort.

"Look at me. Don't close your eyes. I'm coming around to your side." Without waiting for him to respond, I jump out of the Blazer. Obviously, I can't take all my stuff, not if I'm going to have to help Finn walk. I'll come back for the rest later, but I reach in the back, unzip my bag, and grab Mere's compass.

Yanking Finn's door open with one hand, I drag one of his long arms across my neck, then wiggle his legs out and pull him toward me. I wish he'd say something—anything—even something stupid. The cool wind and freezing rain bring him to his senses as I half drag, half lead him up a mound of sand that feels more like Mount Everest.

He finally speaks. "My head hurts like—" His voice breaks off as he doubles over, grabbing his ribs.

I clench my jaw, trying not to collapse under his weight.

"Shh. I've got you. Keep putting one foot in front of the other. We're almost there."

I'm totally lying, but he's not in a position to understand what's going on, much less argue about it. My thighs burn in agony under our combined weight. My wet hoodie sticks to my skin, weighing me down even further. My neck aches from the impact of the airbag and Finn's weight, and I contemplate sitting for a minute or two, but we're still overshadowed by a canopy of drunkenly swaying trees. Peering through the tunnel to the opening at the end of the drive, I spot the shadow of a lopsided bungalow on stilts. The dark outline of a possible shelter, no matter how poorly built, puffs my sails with a second wind.

"Finn. Come on. There's a house up ahead."

The weight across my shoulders lessens a bit when he lifts his head. "Yeah . . ."

He pauses for a second or two after every step to catch his breath. By the time we reach the deck at the top of the stairs, we're drenched through to our skin and shivering against each other. I unpeel his arm from my neck, lean him against the wall near the door, and bang on the window. When no one answers, I wiggle the knob.

Of course, it's locked.

I bang the glass again. Tears burn my eyes. There has to be a key somewhere. When I lean down to look under the mat and find nothing but wood, icy rainwater washes the tears away.

"You're . . . gonna have to break . . ." The howling wind cuts off bits and pieces of his weak speech, but I get the gist of it. Finn wants me to break into this house. I guess it would still be breaking and entering with a key, but it would seem a lot more civilized that way. I survey the windows. Maybe one's unlocked.

A terrifying bang overpowers the groaning of the wind. When I almost jump out of my skin, my foot hits a concrete frog near the door. Somehow, my heart restarts itself after a missed beat.

"Do it," Finn says.

Another bang, and another, cracks the night. I jump again and again. My imagination conjures images of drunk looters with guns shooting up the neighborhood and robbing homes.

"Sophie, it's just . . . the transformers blowing . . ."

Oh, right. Just those little transformers blowing. Nothing to worry about. We're stranded on a narrow strip of land, jutting out into the Atlantic in the middle of an oncoming Category 2 hurricane. Now our only source of power is apparently blowing up as we speak. Clearly, we're perfectly safe—nothing to stress about here, friends.

"Do it," he says a second time.

"Crap, crap, crap," I whisper under my breath.

Curse this boy.

Curse this hurricane.

Curse the transformers.

Curse it all—every last bit of this horrible nightmare.

Bending down, I grab the heavy frog. With a grunt, I heft it to my shoulder, then slam it through the glass.

CHAPTER ELEVEN

A sorrow's crown of sorrow is remembering happier times.

ALFRED, LORD TENNYSON

The house is cold and dark, but it's small, which makes finding the couch easy. I prop Finn in the corner cushions, then head back to the door and the light switch. Flicking the switch does nothing but confirm what Finn already said about the transformers: the power's out. I try a lamp and the TV remote out of desperation. Nothing.

I check my phone for the seventy-fifth time since I got in the car with Finn. Zero signal. Not much battery.

I step back to the couch. Finn's slumped over on his side in a fetal position, teeth chattering. I'm no expert, but I grew up on Dad's forest ranger stories. And it doesn't take a medical degree to realize Finn's headed down a one-way street to shock and maybe even hypothermia if I don't do something fast. Before the situation can spiral any further out of control, I wiggle his shoulder.

He groans and opens his eyes to slits.

"Don't blink. Don't blink," I order in my most authoritative voice as I slide my finger across my phone and switch on the flashlight. When I shine it in his eyes, he winces and blinks. As soon as his eyes obey my command, his pupils constrict to pinpoints under the glare of my flashlight. I know responsive pupils are a good sign that Finn didn't suffer a concussion, and I breathe a sigh of relief.

He rests his arm across his eyes. "Cut the light. It hurts."

"What day is it?"

"That's. A. Stupid. Question." His teeth chatter, chopping up his speech.

"Just tell me." If his pupils are responsive and he's alert to time and place, I can let him sleep for a few hours at a time.

"It's Wednesday. Leave me alone. I'm freezing." He shifts onto his side, clearly settling in for a while.

We really need to get out of our wet clothes.

"Finn!" I grip his shoulder, but he doesn't budge or make a sound. After a few seconds, I take a deep breath and tug his T-shirt down the arm nearest me. Once his elbow clears the armhole, I bend his arm, slipping it inside the body of his shirt. Using the tricks I learned from Mere's rehab nurses, I have him out of his shirt in just a minute. The jeans take longer because they have a button and a zipper. My insides turn all twisty when my fingers brush his stomach. Holding my breath, I stare at the fish mounted over the old fireplace instead of his body. I peel him from his wet jeans inch by inch. Avoiding an underwear malfunction slows me down even further.

When I finally have him stripped down to his SpongeBob boxers, I realize my mistake. He's freezing. Now his whole body moves in rhythm with his chattering teeth. I should have rounded up blankets first. I hate to leave him exposed and cold, but I have to find better supplies.

The kitchen, dining, and living areas are all one room. I push through the closed door opposite the couch. It's a bedroom. Without hesitating, I pull bedspread, blanket, and top sheet off an iron-frame bed with one aggressive yank and head back to Finn. I cover him from chin to toes and carefully tuck the covers in around him. The covers do nothing to lessen the shivering. I need to do something with his wet hair, so I hurry to the tiny L-shaped kitchen in search of dish towels.

I return with an armload of soft towels and hot pads, then drop to my knees beside the couch, thankful Finn appears to have dozed off. As I massage his head with a towel, a bit of color seeps back into his cheeks. When his teeth stop chattering, his face relaxes. He sinks into a deep sleep before my eyes, and something in my chest loosens. It's hard to be irritated with him when he looks so vulnerable—when he's not smirking, when he's not talking.

Maybe Finn's not the real problem. Maybe it's just his mouth. Maybe we'd be great friends if he didn't talk so much, and if we didn't have that little nightmare where he stood me up at the dance. But from what I've seen, the talking will never go away unless someone wires his jaw shut.

Pushing myself to my feet, I head back to the bedroom in search of dry clothes for me. If I'm going to take care of Finn, I need to take care of myself too. The person who owns the house either doesn't spend much time here or is some kind of super minimalist. There's one Crab Shack T-shirt, a pair of men's jeans, an East Carolina sweatshirt, and a pair of flannel drawstring pajama pants. I don't care how cold or wet I am or how incapacitated Finn is, I'd die before prancing around this house anything less than fully clothed.

I take off my wet clothes and tennis shoes, throw on the T-shirt, slip into the way-too-big pj pants that, to my happy surprise, have pockets, and head back to Finn with the jeans and sweatshirt for when he wakes up. He's breathing softly, face still relaxed, so I set to work. I remember this drill from childhood—back when we were still a four-person family with a dad. We rode out many a nor'easter and even a few Category 1 hurricanes. All Outer Banks residents know to be prepared 24/7 for unpredictable weather and power outages. There must be basic storm supplies here somewhere.

The logical place to start is in the kitchen. Trying to take advantage of the last bits of light before I can't see, I pick through the cabinets nearest the back door, methodically opening one, feeling around, and then moving to the next, finding a few cans of soup and other nonperishables as I go. I hit the jackpot when I open the drawer beside the sink—candles, matches, a flashlight, and a value pack of double-A batteries. I set them on the counter and run down my mental checklist.

Shelter—check. Light source—check. Canned goods in the cabinet—check. Water—*crap*.

I try the faucet. A few spurts of water and a bunch of air shoot out, then nothing. We won't make it long without water, so I grab every pot and pan I can find and charge out to the deck, arranging the makeshift buckets in a line near the railing. Securing them with the concrete frog and a couple of heavy flowerpots, I pray they'll withstand the predicted high winds. In an emergency, rainwater might be our only option. Shaking moisture from my hair, I step inside and bolt the door behind me.

There's nothing I can do now but wait for my clothes to dry, wait for Finn to wake, and listen to the rising wind. The house sways a little, and I remind myself that's what it's designed to do. The stilts do more than elevate the living space above water level; they also provide some give in strong winds. Staring into the blackness beyond the window, I tell myself I've got this. I'm pretty good at taking care of myself and everyone else. The boy sleeping soundly in the cocoon of warm blankets and sheets at my back is evidence of that.

But guilt nibbles at my insides. I should be taking care of Mom and Mere, not Finn. I should have told Mom about my tires. Maybe all of this could have been avoided if I had.

Sadly, there's nothing else I can do to improve our situation right now. I don't want to waste our light sources, so I sit in the dark, listening to Finn's steady breathing. I draft a mental to-do list of what needs to be done at daybreak and pray the storm will turn back out to the Atlantic. Or maybe some emergency personnel will find us on their door-to-door rounds.

A loud bang cracks the side of the house, and my head snaps. I realize I must have closed my eyes for a second and that debris is hitting the house, probably a trash can or lawn chair or something someone forgot to put away or tie down. My butt's numb from sitting on the hardwood floor, and my whole body aches. Common sense tells me to get some sleep, but my stubborn streak insists I stay alert—stay focused. When I yawn, I realize common sense is going to win.

I debate going to the bedroom, but I worry something could happen if Finn and I are separated, even by a wall. It's like that reality show where people have to survive naked in the wilderness for weeks at a time. They may fight like crazy, but anything is better than being alone. Finn's the last person I'd choose to be stranded with, but he's all I've got. And anybody is better than nobody.

I push myself to standing and arch my aching lower back. My spine pops. I survey the darkness again. We're surrounded by windows. If the winds bear down even harder, we'll have to move to a closet or the corner of the kitchen away from the threat of breaking glass. I gently sit on the edge of the couch in the bend behind Finn's knees and kind of recline on the arm of the couch. I don't have to touch anything but his calves and feet, which seems safe enough—no room for misinterpretation.

Trying to be very still, I rest my head against the back of the couch and concentrate on the wind. At some point I must have fallen into a deep sleep, or I'm still dreaming, because I'm nestled in blankets and . . . warm. And the world on the other side of my closed eyelids is no longer black. It's more charcoal gray.

I exhale, savoring one second of perfect quiet and warmth. Then soft laughter rips me to awareness. My eyes fly open.

Inches from my face is another face—a smiling face, framed by messy, towel-dried black hair.

"Morning, Sunshine." Finn winks at me. The goose egg on his forehead has already turned a greenish-gray.

My body stiffens. "Did the storm miss us?" I ask between mostly closed lips, praying he found the sweatshirt and jeans I laid out for him. If I weren't swaddled like a baby, I'd yank my hand to my mouth. I can only imagine the dragon breath I must have this morning. I wouldn't wish it on my worst enemy.

"No, I don't think we've seen the worst yet. But we'll be okay. The house is pretty well built." He moves slowly and carefully, like an old man, as he pushes himself up to a sitting position on the edge of the couch. He seems completely unfazed by the proximity of his body to mine.

I, on the other hand, can barely breathe.

"I want to say thanks," he says, changing the subject and saving me from the awkward silence.

"For what?" I haven't done anything. Maybe the bang to his head scrambled more than his face.

Turning sideways to face me, he playfully bumps my hip with his elbow, then lowers one eyebrow. His face is serious, but his eyes are speckled with mischief. "Uh, let's see. For the blankets, for the supplies I saw on the counter, for the pots on the deck, for the clothes . . ."

Thank you, God. Thank you. At least he's dressed.

"Thank you for saving me," he says.

"It was nothing." Anyone would have done the same thing in a similar situation.

Now even his eyes are serious. "It was *something*. I should have listened to you. It's my fault we're stranded. I'm sorry. Good thing you're like some kind of ninja-survivor girl."

Now I'm the one laughing—like a real, genuine laugh—which is completely absurd, considering the situation we're facing with the weather.

If the forecast hasn't changed, we could be in for a direct hit sometime in the next few hours, which means we have plans to prepare, decisions to make, and actions to take. And no time to lie around laughing like friends . . . or like anything else.

But for a second, laughing with Finn doesn't seem so bad.

CHAPTER TWELVE

*A life that is half-truth
is the darkest lie of all.*

ALFRED, LORD TENNYSON

Several hours pass as we wait to see what else the hurricane has in store. My phone hasn't had service since yesterday, and Finn's watch is no help. It must be at least midmorning. Maybe even noon. It's hard to say since the sky never advanced past slate-gray. Our cottage on stilts remains shrouded in gloom. We eat lukewarm chicken noodle soup I heat over a couple of candles.

"Won't your parents be worried about you?" I ask between bites.

He slurps a spoonful of squishy noodles and shrugs. "It's just me and my mom."

I could have sworn I remembered a mom *and* dad at school functions. Maybe his parents separated too. "Isn't that even more reason for her to worry?"

He leans forward to set his empty bowl on the driftwood table in front of the couch. The casual movement seems dreamlike with the sun camouflaged, the wind howling, and the house swaying beneath us. "She loves me. She worries, but we both learned one thing when my dad died—life is meant to be lived. *Really* lived. Like, suck every last drop of life out of life every day because today could be your last. That's why we moved back here—to be closer to Zeke and to the ocean."

A speck of chicken lodges in my throat. I had no idea he'd lost his dad. It must have been after he moved away. I just kind of figured from his happy-go-lucky attitude that he was like Yesenia, that he'd never come face-to-face with any of the big bad *D*s—disability, divorce, death. The smile on his face doesn't match his death and dying comments, if you ask me. But he's not really asking me. I'm caught once again by the oxymoron that is Finn Sanders. His words are those of a wise old sage, but his face is more impish, stand-up comic.

"And she knew I might hang out with Zeke," he says.

When a Christmas-tree-size pine branch slaps the window, I jerk, sloshing soup out of the bowl. The wind is picking up.

I set my bowl beside his and begin grabbing the books and blankets I've piled up around us. "It's time," I say.

Without arguing, he stands. When he reaches for the flashlight and batteries on the table, he struggles to catch his breath. I stop to look at him, see his hand extended but frozen in place.

"You okay?" I ask.

"Yeah. Fine."

He's lying. The grimace on his face and the hand squeezing his ribs speak way louder than his hoarse voice.

"You're hurt."

"I'm fine." As if to prove it, he releases his side and grabs the flashlight and batteries.

I don't move until he nudges me toward the bedroom. It's a good thing the closet is on the interior wall and even better that it's pretty much empty. I fold the sheets and blankets to fit the floor. He grabs pillows from the bed. By the time we finish, we have a cozy hidey-hole I would have killed for back in elementary school. We have the books and a deck of cards I found with the emergency candles and other storm supplies.

"You take this thing everywhere you go?" He flicks Mere's compass, which I have hung around my neck.

I stand outside looking in, hoping he'll go first. For some reason, retreating to the closet seems like a big decision, like crossing some sort of invisible line, like an admission that our lives are at stake. "My sister's really attached to it," I say without explaining that Dad gave it to Mere, or that it was the only thing she hung on to after the accident, or that Mom and I packed our compasses away long ago. It's not like we'll have the money anytime soon to travel somewhere that requires orienteering equipment.

Finn leaves it at that, dramatically gesturing for me to enter. "*Mi casa es su casa.*"

I try to smile, but I don't like it. I don't want to be trapped in a closet at the mercy of this stupid storm. But we have no choice, so I cross the threshold.

"Wait!" He grabs my shoulder.

"What?" I jump back, positive he's spotted a black widow or some mammoth rodent.

"We forgot the most important provision." He backs out of the room.

I examine the dim closet. We've got everything that was on my list to get us through tonight and into tomorrow. We agreed candles and matches would be too dangerous. We agreed canned goods would be too messy, which is why we ate before the retreat and stashed only a box of saltine crackers and a bag of gluten-free rice cakes in the closet.

I try to ignore the rain pelting the house harder than ever. These are not the plump drops of a summer storm. These raindrops are sharper, longer, more like miniature knives than precipitation. Hugging myself, I rub my upper arms and try not to think about wind, or rain, or knives.

As I wait for Finn to return, it hits me that this might be my last chance to pee for a really long time. When I scurry back from the bathroom, he's hiding something behind his back.

"Ta-da!" he announces, whipping out a box of Twinkies.

"How old are they?" I scrunch up my face.

"Who knows? Who cares? These things have enough preservatives to survive the apocalypse with the mutant cockroaches. And they're yummy." He places his fingers on my lower back, coaxing me forward.

I step inside again and plop down cross-legged at one end of the closet. He holds his side as he lowers himself to the floor at the opposite end. Sliding off his flip-flops, he stretches out his long legs. When he does, his toes brush my knee. The skin beneath my flannel pants tingles.

"Now what?" I ask, pulling the door shut on its creaky hinges and clicking the flashlight to its lowest setting.

"Truth or dare?"

I shake my head and try not to squirm under his gaze. "Maybe we could just rest for a little while." I lean my head back against the wall and close my eyes without waiting for him to respond.

The minutes creep into hours. The afternoon passes mostly in silence. My butt hurts. If we don't *do* something, I'm going to go stir crazy. "You want to play cards?" I ask.

He scans the closet dramatically. "I'd suggest spin the bottle, but there are only two of us and no bottle. How about high-stakes blackjack?"

I pull my knees toward my chest. "Um, I was thinking rummy."

"Boring." He picks up the deck of cards, then shuffles in the dim light without glancing down.

"I like rummy." I wrap my arms around my bent knees.

"Exactly."

"What's that supposed to mean?" I ask, my voice a little too loud in the cramped space.

"Nothing." He drums his fingers on the cards thoughtfully. "It just seems like you can't have fun if you never try anything new."

"I try new things." I unclasp my arms, sit up a bit, and lift my chin.

"Like what?" He shuffles the cards again, arches the deck, pushes them together, taps them on his leg, then repeats.

"I tried German last year."

"Oh! Wow! That was daring."

I don't need a lot of light to see the mischief in his eyes. Gritting my teeth, I decide not to rise to his bait.

"You weren't this uptight in ninth grade." He nudges my knee with his bare foot. "What happened?"

A muscle twitches in my jaw.

"Have I done something to offend you?" He finally gives the cards a rest.

Inhaling, I pause to check my words. Is he so inconsiderate that he's forgotten he stood me up? Or is he so insensitive that he has no idea how that would affect me—or any girl?

"Of course not," I lie, not wanting him to know how much I cared about the whole dance thing back in ninth grade and definitely not wanting to go into everything that's happened to my family in the last two years.

"Are you sure?"

"I'm sure. I'm just really stressed out, okay?" I force myself to meet his eyes.

"Okay," he says, interrupting my thoughts and handing me the deck of cards. "If you won't play blackjack, I guess rummy's better than nothing."

The cards are warm from his hands, and the deck's too thin. I start counting. "We're missing cards."

"It doesn't matter. Just deal." When he gestures for me to begin, his hand brushes mine.

I press my back against the wall and pull my feet toward me. "We're missing seven cards. We can't play rummy with that many missing cards."

"Dang." He snaps his fingers. "I guess that means no strip poker either."

"Darn." I drop my shoulders and smile in spite of myself.

"I guess we'll just have to play truth or dare, then." He grabs the box of Twinkies off the floor and rips open one end.

"I think we're a little old for truth or dare." I shake my head when he offers me one of the spongy torpedoes of sugar.

"Actually, it's a good icebreaker. Scientific evidence proves that people who know each other and feel comfortable together make better teams, especially in adverse situations. I think a hurricane qualifies as an adverse situation." He looks down his nose at me, like Mr. Richards does at a defiant student.

"Fine," I say, slightly taken aback by such technical reasoning to play a children's game. I'd rather sleep, or read, or have my wisdom teeth removed, but I don't want to hear another lecture on trying new things or answer any questions about my chilly behavior.

"You go first. Truth or dare?" He bites off half a Twinkie.

"Truth." I set my jaw, daring him to taunt me.

He smirks but doesn't comment on my choice. Seconds tick by as he scratches his chin. He's enjoying making me wait. "Got it. What's a secret talent nobody knows you have?"

"I can diagram sentences."

"Everyone knows you can diagram sentences."

"No, I can *really* diagram sentences."

When he lowers one eyebrow, his bottom lip shifts to the side, like he's thinking hard. "I don't know—"

"I can diagram the Pledge of Allegiance in fifty-seven seconds." I cross my arms.

"Impressive." He nods.

"Truth or dare?"

"Dare." More smirking.

Of. Course.

Ha! I smile as I reach behind the small stack of books against the wall. His confidence falters. Mine grows as I dangle the bag of gluten-free rice cakes back and forth in front of his face.

"The whole bag, buddy. The *whole* bag." For someone trapped in a closet, during an oncoming hurricane, I'm enjoying this a bit too much.

"Fine." He snatches the bag from my hands.

I lean back against the wall, cross my arms, and settle in to enjoy the show.

He untwists the tie, then lowers his nose to the partially open bag to take a whiff. His face screws up. "They smell like dirt."

"It's called real food."

He shoves an entire round in his mouth. A speck of puffed rice flies toward me as he shoves in a second and a third.

"Truth or dare?" he asks, holding the last cake near his mouth.

"Truth."

He swallows, then pauses dramatically before continuing. "Most embarrassing moment?"

That's easy. Waiting for a boy to show up for the ninth-grade dance with flowers in my hair and a dreamy smile on my face.

"Ummm . . ." I pluck the last rice cake from his hand to kill time.

His eyes remain locked on mine as he wipes a stray crumb from the corner of his mouth.

"Tracking horse manure onto the bus in fifth grade." I'm not being completely dishonest. The horse poop thing was really embarrassing. Kids called me Stinky Sophie for weeks.

"Truth or dare?" I ask.

"Dare." He smiles and does that cool-chin-jerk thing guys do.

"Lick the bottom of your flip-flop." I smile my super-sweet-little-church-girl smile.

Without hesitation, he reaches for his flip-flop.

"Stop." I smack his hand out of the way. "This is stupid. You'll do anything. I can lie, and you won't know the difference."

"Will I really do anything?" He peaks his fingers and squints one eye.

"You will."

"Okay, then give me a truth."

I don't want to play anymore, but I'm curious to know some of his secrets too. "What's *your* most embarrassing moment?" I ask.

"There are so many." He shrugs.

"Are you scared?" I contemplate feeling guilty, taunting him like that, but then I remind myself I'm not doing anything to him that he hasn't done to me.

This time he rubs his chin. "Probably that time I went to school with a hot dog in my pocket and the cops came with the drug dogs to search the building. The dogs went crazy, and everyone assumed I had drugs."

Oh my gosh! I had completely forgotten about the peculiar incident of Finn Sanders and the illicit hot dog. I meet his eyes and smile. When I do, I remember something else I had forgotten. He used to walk dogs at the Humane Society and foster them at his house. He had a beagle named Annie for months. The dog had thunder phobia, separation anxiety, and a bee allergy, but a passion for processed meat, especially bologna and hot dogs. He took her everywhere with him to socialize her. He would apologize to strangers in the pet store if she had a fear-incited accident and clean up after her without complaining. Our love of dogs was one of the things other than chess we had in common. And I'd completely forgotten about it.

I shake my head and try to change the subject again. "Let's read instead. Okay?" I hate the weak sound of my voice as I lift the stack of paperbacks to my lap.

"Whatever you say, Bookworm."

As I sift through the books, he sits up straighter. He looks all studious, but I know he's mocking me.

"*Deliverance?*" I hold up a yellowed paperback with a couple of commando-looking dudes on the cover.

"Way too dark for the circumstances." He snaps the rubber band securing the deck of cards.

"*The Last Song?*" I hold up a book with an almost-kissing couple on the cover, but I already know no self-respecting teenage boy would pick the Nicholas Sparks book.

"Don't those books always have sad endings?"

"Yeah. Somebody usually dies . . ." My voice trails off when I realize I've circled back to the subject I'd hoped to leave back in the living room.

His brow furrows. "There's a difference between sadness and dying, Sophie."

Straightening the blanket near the baseboard, I wait for him to go all mystical philosopher on me. Whether or not I meant to, I did bring this on myself.

"Sadness is being stuck. Not pursuing your dreams. Sacrificing. Compromising. Death can be really beautiful."

I try to look unconcerned, but I feel my face quivering, threatening to cave in on itself. My knuckles whiten against the blue book in my hand. Tears salt behind my eyes. I'm not sure whether I want to cry or hit something.

Losing someone you love is not beautiful.

Period.

"What else you got?" he asks, almost as if he can read my mind. Almost as if he knows I *need* him to change the subject.

"Stephen King." I hold up a book with a horrific clown on the front. "Somebody named Dean Koontz and a biography about some guy—Henry Van Dyke."

He reaches for the King novel. "Yes! *It*. My favorite."

"If guys being hunted in the woods is too dark, I'm pretty sure demonic clowns are too. The biography looks—"

"Safest."

"Well, it does." I shrug. The wind howls. Something scrapes across the roof, reinforcing my point. "I just don't think we need anything to put us further on edge."

"It's fine. You don't need to explain. Henry Van Dyke it is. I think we studied him in Lit." He rests his head on the wall behind him and rubs his side. "I'd kill for some beef jerky."

I ignore the jerky comment. "I didn't study him in my Lit class. I'd remember."

"I'm pretty sure I did." He closes his eyes. Clearly, the debate isn't worth his energy. "Just read. Okay?"

The first page reads like a history textbook, basically tracing Van Dyke's life from infancy through school. On the second page, I have to raise my voice a little. The rising wind is an unwelcome reminder of the serious situation outside the sanctuary of the closet. The author goes on to explain Van Dyke's work as an author and pastor. Chapter one ends with a long list of his songs, poems, and short stories.

I pause, listening for Finn's breathing over the racket outside. Nothing. But I see his sides rise and fall in a relaxed rhythm. He's asleep. I'm pretty sure it would take a gallon of allergy medicine or an elephant tranquilizer to put me to sleep right now. Yet he's totally unfazed by the threat of the hurricane.

I flip ahead a couple of chapters in hopes that Mr. Van Dyke's story picks up. Maybe he had scandalous affairs or addiction problems like so many famous writers. I need something to keep me distracted, especially if Finn isn't awake to do so, so I continue to read aloud.

My voice rises, battling the storm. By page twenty-seven, I'm pretty certain Van Dyke has no skeletons hiding in any of his closets. Chapter three closes with an inscription he wrote for a sundial to be placed in a friend's garden: "Time is Too Slow for those who Wait, Too Swift for those who Fear, Too Long for those who Grieve . . ."

I pause mid-poem to digest the words. They're familiar, but I have no idea where I've heard them. Maybe it's a text Lit teachers use. Maybe Finn's right. Much to my dismay, he frequently is. Maybe I did read Van Dyke for school.

Without opening his eyes, Finn finishes the last lines. "Too Short for those who Rejoice; But for those who Love, Time is not."

I close the book. "Is it from Lit?"

He shakes his head.

"Where?" I uncross my legs, straightening them alongside his down the center of the closet.

"My dad's funeral."

I don't respond. Thankfully, I don't have to.

"My dad picked it. Mom loved it. The preacher agreed it would be perfect. It's true if you think about it." When I still don't respond, he opens his eyes. "You don't believe me about the beautiful death thing, do you?"

I can't lie. Honestly, I can't speak, so I just lift my shoulders in a noncommittal shrug and pray he changes the subject.

"When we found out he wasn't going to beat the colon cancer, we made a pact to enjoy the time we had left." His eyes bore into mine.

I can't look away, so I open my big fat mouth. "I thought colon cancer was pretty treatable." Okay, that was stupid and insensitive.

"It usually is if you catch it early. His doctors didn't suspect it, though, because he was young, and healthy, and had a high tolerance to pain. By the time they did, it had spread. That's why we moved—for an experimental treatment in Charlottesville."

I refuse to open my mouth, refuse to spew some stupid medical thing I've read on the Internet, refuse to say anything about a stupid ninth-grade dance that suddenly seems trivial in the face of the loss he suffered. I bite the inside of my cheek instead.

"He had something called Lynch syndrome. Anyway, at the very end, he had to go to hospice for pain meds. They said he'd only make it a few days. He made it closer to a few weeks. Eventually, Mom and I had to take shifts. Life goes on outside even when someone you love is dying."

He isn't telling me anything I don't know. I mean, Mere isn't dead in the real sense of the word, but the big sister I knew and loved is gone forever. Granted, she's still physically alive, and I adore her, and I would do anything for her. But she's a different person now. She'll never dance again. She's not the big sister who ended the Stinky Sophie comments when I couldn't end them myself, or the sister who taught me how to apply eyeliner, and definitely not the daredevil who taught me to run barrels on old Jack. And I'm not the little sister urging Jack into tight turns at breakneck speed either.

In a weird way I can't even explain, her survival makes things more confusing. To people who didn't know Mere very well, there she is in her physical body, alive. They see an emotionally flat young woman who lacks physical coordination and seems to struggle with short-term memory issues. And there's nothing wrong with that, but that's not the sister I grew up with. She was a whirlwind of joy who left everyone she met floating in a wake of delight. She moved like a swan or a cheetah, depending on her mood.

Losing Mere as I knew her was the worst part of the accident for me. Part of me ended with her that day. My world got knocked out of orbit, but everybody else's lives, even Yesenia's, just kind of went along like nothing happened—like a gnat died, not my big sister. The doctors told us to be thankful she was alive, to create a new life for her and for ourselves. And we'd been trying, and I've been so thankful she's here.

But now I realize I'm still grieving.

Hard.

Sitting alone with Finn in a closet in the middle of a hurricane, I start to grasp what my school counselor has been trying to tell me for months. An idea swirls in my head like a cloud. It's there. I can see it, but if I reach for it, my hand goes right through. Are Finn and my evolving awareness of my feelings somehow connected?

After a long pause, Finn continues. "I was sitting in Algebra, near the end of ninth grade, at a new school. Dad had been at hospice for a while, but all of a sudden I just had to be there. I called Zeke to get me. As much as he hates leaving home, he drove all the way up to Virginia. We swung by the house and I grabbed a shoe box of pictures. When we got there, nothing had changed. Dad was unconscious like he had been for days. But instead of Mom leaving me with him while she went to return calls or shower or whatever she needed to do, she stayed." He stares at the wall above my head, reliving the memory. He smiles like he's talking about a wedding or a family reunion, not his father's death.

I sit frozen in place, hoping he won't notice my watery eyes or trembling lip. He covers my hand with his, and I realize he sees the eyes, the lip, and possibly a whole lot more. Oddly, I don't pull away. We sit for a second, hands touching. I try to remember the last time I intentionally touched anyone other than Mom, Mere, or Yesenia, but I honestly can't remember. Then something scrapes across the shingles, like fingernails on a chalkboard, and I slide my hand away.

Finn picks up where he left off. "The three of us scooted chairs up to the bed. I pulled some of my favorite pictures out of the shoe box. Dad fishing with Grandpa off the Nags Head pier. Mom shoving cake in Dad's mouth at their wedding. Me on his shoulders playing chicken at the pool. Zeke told a story about this psychotic dog that bit Dad in the butt. Mom told the story about how she threw up on their first date. We laughed a lot. The stories just kind of wound down. The sun was setting as I closed the shoe box."

He draws in a long, slow breath, then meets my eyes. "As soon as I closed the box and our laughter ended, Dad's breathing hitched. My mom told him it was okay to go. The three of us held hands around his bed. Zeke was singing 'Amazing Grace,' and then Dad just left us. I don't know how to explain it, but it was peaceful. I've never felt anything like it. All I can say is if that's what it's like to die, there's nothing to be afraid of."

He looks at my crossed arms and tilted jaw. "What?" he asks.

"You're not the only one who's experienced a loss, Finn." I pick a piece of lint off my pants. "And maybe it left you feeling all warm and fuzzy, but it ruined my family."

For once, he doesn't speak. He just sits there, waiting for me to continue—no smart-aleck comments, no Zen Buddhism. And once again, I open my mouth. I'm not sure if it's because of the dropping barometric pressure, the tug of the full moon, or just being locked in a closet with Finn Sanders during a hurricane.

"My sister was the center of our family. She was like a people magnet—old people, young people, you name it. They all loved her." Despite my racing pulse and fists, I continue. "I loved her—I still love her . . ." My voice cracks.

Finn sits like a hunter in a tree stand, hyper-focused on my face and perfectly still—like I'm a deer at the edge of a clearing, alert and ready to bolt at the first sign of danger.

But I don't bolt. I barrel ahead. "But my big sister never got her chance *to suck every drop of life out of life*." I pause to let him hear how ridiculous his words sound twisted and thrown back in his face.

"What happened?" he asks, his voice so quiet I can't be certain whether he said it or just mouthed the words.

Normally, this is where I would shut down, drop the steel door on my emotions, block out anyone and everyone—even Yesenia. But for some unexplainable reason, my mouth barrels ahead of my self-control.

"They were on their way home from the feed store on the mainland. Dad texted to say there was an accident on the bypass, and they were taking the beach road. Nobody knows for sure what happened next. All I know for sure is Dad hit a dump truck head-on. They had to cut him and my sister out of the car. They said it was a miracle they survived the impact. Dad walked away with a broken arm and some cuts and bruises, the other guy without a scratch. But we didn't know if Meredith would live. She did, but she had a TBI—" I skip the part about the truck driver accusing Dad of texting and driving. The police verified Dad's last text was sent several minutes *before* the crash. No charges were filed. Dad never talked about what he was doing with his phone at the time of the accident, and we never asked. The guilt was already eating at him. It seemed too cruel and too judgmental to push the subject despite the rumors that his forest ranger connections with local law enforcement might have encouraged the cops to look the other way.

Finn shakes his head, and I remember not everyone knows as much about the human brain as I do.

"She had a traumatic brain injury." I swallow, forcing myself to look at him. It's still hard for me to talk about it. "As if that wasn't bad enough, the day after the wreck she had a stroke. The doctors think it was a result of the trauma to the blood vessels in her brain. It messed her up—bad. She had to relearn how to walk, and swallow, and all sorts of horrible stuff. And it changed her. She was no longer the prima ballerina of our family, dancing her way through life. She was depressed and angry." My voice cracks again. "She'll never be the—"

Now I'm the one tilting my head back and closing my eyes.

It has nothing to do with my chill attitude and everything to do with trying not to cry.

He places a hand on my knee. This time I stiffen. I didn't tell him my story for sympathy. I told it to prove my point.

"Sophie, I'm sorry," he whispers.

I count to ten, then open my eyes. His face swims in my blurry vision. When I look at him, I believe him. He doesn't say *at least she's alive* or any of the other stupid things people tried to tell me after the accident.

There's no laughter in his eyes. He's not opening his mouth to argue his point. I don't know how to explain it. He just—*is*. He's in the moment, not fighting me, not fighting anything—just still and quiet . . . and serious.

Something else is weird. I don't feel exactly relaxed; it's definitely not peace. But it's like the fist gripping my chest unclenched a little when I shared my story out loud. It's like every muscle fiber in my body has been tight as a piano wire for so long, I forgot what it felt like to not be rigid.

Then glass shatters outside the closet, and whatever was happening to me—whatever was happening between us—is gone.

We sit frozen in place.

Listening.

What we hear is much, much worse than driving rain or gale-force winds.

CHAPTER THIRTEEN

*The night comes on that
knows not morn . . .*

ALFRED, LORD TENNYSON

s that what I think it is?" I ask, shaking my head. We sit
in the closet, paralyzed. I pray I'm wrong. Pray the water I
hear is pounding rain or the sound of the ocean carried toward
us on the wind. Pray it's not what I think it is.

But Finn nods and grabs my hand. I scoot toward him. I
know what he's going to say before he opens his mouth. "It's the
waves. Storm surge. We must be closer to shore than we realized."

Not good.

Not. Good. At. All.

I squeeze my eyes shut. This cannot be happening. I have
no idea what time it is—maybe eight or nine. We've been in
this closet for what feels like forever, or all day at the least. It's
night again—maybe a little over twenty-four hours since Mom
and Mere left for Williamston. Mom must be worried sick.
And it's my fault. I thought I had everything under control. I
should have found Jim sooner. I should have done something
about my tires. I shouldn't have wasted time cleaning up trash.

"It's waves. We've got to move." He shoves on his flip-flops, and then pulls me to my feet, interrupting the thoughts spiraling in my head. We duck to avoid banging our heads on the hanging rod above us.

I lace on my still-damp shoes, thankful I thought to place them with the closet rations, then grab the compass hanging around my neck and tuck it inside my shirt. Seconds later, Finn pushes the closet door open. With the windows shattered on this side of the house and no door to muffle the sound, the ocean crashes, churns, and growls. I picture greedy waves devouring the dunes and our little sanctuary perched on the brink of disaster. If the house goes, we go. Finn and I both know the storm surge is a thousand times more powerful and deadly than the wind. If it gets a hold of us, we're toast—waterlogged toast.

Finn grabs the flashlight, pulling me through the living room. When he turns the knob on the door leading to the deck, the force of the wind slams it into his chest.

"Look out," he screams, then ducks his head and pulls me out into the storm.

We fight the wind to the deck rail and peer down into the dark. As my eyes adjust to the gloom, I realize the clumps of white creeping beneath the house aren't sand. They're sea foam, frothing ahead of the approaching surge of waves.

"We're going to have to run for it," he shouts over the wind.

"Where?" I ask, cupping my hand above my eyes to block out the shards of rain ripping at my face.

He pulls me toward the stairs leading down to the carport. "Farther inland. Anywhere."

He and I both know the dangers. We've heard the stories

of vehicles washed away by twelve inches of flood water moving a few miles per hour. We don't know the terrain, and it's pitch black. It wouldn't take much of an accident to cause a slip. We could be separated in an instant and one or both of us dragged out to sea, or whacked in the head with floating debris, or electrocuted by downed power lines in the water.

I shiver, and it's not from the freezing rain. Tightening my grip on his hand, I scurry after him down the stairs. Icy water rushes over my foot when I step down to the concrete pad under the house, and my flannel pajama pants twist around my ankles like gnarled hands. The ocean thunders around us from every direction. Hunched forward, hands clasped, we run headlong down the driveway. In a matter of minutes, we've gone from safe hidey-hole to out of control. What I thought was our sanctuary morphed into a deathtrap.

When Finn stops short, I slam into his back and remember to breathe.

My drenched shirt presses against his drenched shirt. The wind and rain drown out his next words, but he points at a fallen pine tree blocking our path. The thing could've killed us if it had fallen on our way to the house. He steps up onto the trunk and hops down on the far side. I press my hand against the lump under my shirt. I will not lose Mere's compass. It's my last link to her and Mom. Even if it's only a symbolic connection, I'm holding on to it for dear life.

Finn shouts something else I can't understand, but I get the gist of what he's trying to communicate from his hand gestures. He wants us to follow the yellow line in the middle of the road. I kind of want to follow him, but he's heading north—back the way we came. The houses spread out farther north, which means less chance for shelter. It seems illogical to head that way. We should head south toward civilization, where we're more likely to run into people riding out the storm or emergency personnel.

When he tugs on my hand a second time, I still don't budge. He turns to face me, eyes wide, rivers of water running down his face.

He leans in to my ear, shouting over the wind. "There's a volunteer fire department a few miles north, and Zeke's that way."

I want to argue, but his point about the volunteer fire department makes sense. They'll be first to get back power, phone service, and water after the storm. I compromise, telling myself this will go better than his *back-roads-will-save-time* reasoning, despite the painful twisting in my stomach.

We head north, bent at the waist like mountain climbers as we fight the wind. I have no idea how far we've gone. If I had to guess, not very far. Every step is a battle.

I study the ground immediately in front of my feet as we struggle forward. The second time Finn stops, I catch myself before barreling into him. He's pointing at a mailbox. Squinting, I try to read his lips.

"A house!" he shouts.

And he's right. A very large, very expensive, very sturdy house squats on a rise to our left, maybe a couple hundred yards farther inland than the last cottage. A glimmer of hope lights in my chest. Shaking a fist at the black sky, I tilt my head back and smile.

We're saved.

Our hope reignited, we move faster than before up a small rise to the large house sitting atop a four-car garage. As we approach, Finn grabs my hand and gestures up to the front windows. There appears to be a flickering light inside—a lantern maybe. I should be thrilled. But something about the quivering light and the horizontal sheets of rain in the dark night makes me shiver.

Cursing Dad and Mere for the horror movie marathons Mom never knew about, I shake off the worry. Where there is light without power, there must be humans. Where there are humans, there must be adults. There can't be any other teenagers trapped alone in this storm. That only happens in scary movies, and this is not a scary movie. This is as real as it gets. Plus, Finn doesn't seem worried as he drags me up the steps to the expansive deck that wraps around the entire house.

Where the roof extends over the front door, the wind isn't quite as piercing. I can hear Finn when he speaks.

"We made it, Bookworm!" He squeezes my shoulder, giving me a little shake.

As he lifts his heavy flashlight to bang on the door, I smile. "Yeah, we did."

After a few quick raps, the door swings open. A wide-eyed man older than my father stares at us. His eyes survey us one at a time and head to toe. Under other circumstances, he might frighten me. Under these circumstances, his sturdy house and massive lantern offer a promise of refuge from the weather. Besides, inviting two strangers into his home must be more of a risk for him than going in is for us.

When he gestures for us to enter, we scurry across the threshold. He shuts the door behind us, blocking out much of the noise from the storm.

"What are you two doing out in this?" he barks, then levels

his eyes on me. Something about his jittery eyes makes me nervous.

He wipes a sheen of sweat or rain—I can't be sure which—from his forehead.

"We wrecked," Finn says, seeming to sense my uneasiness.

I appreciate him answering and drawing the man's attention away from me. I glance around the high-ceilinged room as they talk and realize the house is made mostly of walls of glass. It's just as huge as it looked from the road but not nearly as sturdy, and the roof is already leaking in several places. To make matters worse, the man has lit candles all over the place, which everyone who knows anything about hurricanes knows is a major *no no*—it's the number one cause of fires during power outages.

The fear in my gut flares. Dad always said, "The key ingredients to handling any crisis are a clear plan and a calm head." This guy doesn't seem to have either.

Finn's eyes meet mine. He seems to be able to read my thoughts. "Maybe we should find a place with less glass farther inland," he says to the man.

"No!" the man growls, deep and low.

I take a step back.

Finn reaches a hand in front of his chest. It hits me that he looks way more adult than the adult in this situation. "You know the saying—run from water, hide from wind."

"What does it look like I'm doing?" The man gestures wildly around the room. "I'm inside, away from the wind."

"But all this glass is going to go eventually," Finn reasons.

"I'm not leaving. I sunk my life savings into this place, and I'm staying here to protect it."

Finn tries to speak. "Please—"

"Listen, kid. If you know everything, why don't you move on?"

Finn opens his mouth. When he does, a gust of wind whooshes under the crack in the door. A candle falls on the couch and smolders. The man rushes past me to snuff it out.

"It will be ruined!" he says as he beats the small flames into submission. "That couch cost five grand."

Finn looks at me, eyebrows raised in question. I know what he's thinking; this man is losing it. He doesn't realize the danger of his candles, and he's way more concerned about a couch than his own life.

"Let's go," I say.

Nodding, Finn grabs my hand and pulls me to the door.

"Hey, kids." The man raises a fist at us. "You and your friends better stay away after the storm. There won't be any looting around here."

My insides churn like the storm. I'm relieved to say goodbye to this irrational man with the wild eyes and the hazardous candles. At the same time, I'm terrified to face what an enraged Mother Nature has in store for us outside.

Finn shakes his head at the man. As he leads me toward the door, I bite my lip and pray for better luck at the next house.

CHAPTER FOURTEEN

But the tender grace of a day that is dead Will never come back to me.

ALFRED, LORD TENNYSON

Now we're back where we started, trudging up the middle of the dark road and searching for shelter. The lack of sleep, stress overload, and storm effects must be making me delirious, because when the *doo-doo-DOO-doo* of the *Twilight Zone* theme song buzzes in my head, irrational laughter wells in my throat. I feel like we've been sucked through time and space into some low-quality black-and-white movie.

My calf muscles complain as we plod forward, reminding me this is no joke. I know Mom and Mere must be worried sick, and Mom's friend Carla too.

"Look out," Finn shouts as he jumps to the right.

But the wind is loud, and I'm so distracted that I don't move out of the way fast enough. Something whacks me in the shin. A beer bottle maybe. I scream through gritted teeth. I know I scream because the noise vibrates inside my head, but I can't hear it with my ears.

"Are you—" Before he finishes, something else grazes my shoulder.

It doesn't hurt like the bottle to the shin, so I press forward. As a warm rush of liquid pours down my arm, I realize I've got a problem. Finn turns back to me, his face hovering inches above mine. Concern registers in his eyes as he shines the flashlight he's been preserving on my cold face. He looks like something out of a scary movie with its light flickering on his wet face, eyes wide, mouth open, his black hair whipping in the wind like Medusa's snakes. When he lowers the flashlight to my shoulder, a pink stain spreads like spilled fruit punch across my shirt. And there's a lot of pink. I backpedal as he reaches toward my neck.

"Stop, Sophie. Let me see it," he shouts over the wind. The muscles in his cheek twitch as he pushes the flashlight into my hands. With both his hands free, he reaches toward my collarbone. I follow his movement with the light. When I spot the jagged shard protruding from the soft spot between my neck and shoulder, my knees go weak. It's hard to tell, but it looks like the twisted lid of a soup can. My God, the thing could have pierced my jugular. I could have . . . could have . . . died—bled out in the middle of an empty road in the center of the hurricane straight from Hades.

I blink, trying to keep my blurry world in focus. I will not pass out—will not pass out.

Finn grips my head in both his hands, then leans in to me. His lips brush the edge of my ear when he speaks. "That's got to come out."

Closing my eyes, I shake my head. Uh-uh. Not happening. I've seen this sort of thing in movies, and I'm pretty sure the person bleeds out when the arrow or knife or whatever is removed. The pink spreading down my arm and abdomen is bad enough. Spurts of blood would send me over the brink to hysteria. The wind changes directions suddenly, and I stagger. He tightens his grip on me.

"I know what you're thinking." The set of his jaw and the tone in his voice command my attention.

The boy gripping my face in his strong hands shares zero resemblance to the class clown I'm used to. Now he's all hardcore, one hundred percent rescuer doing everything he can to save me. I appreciate his help, but I need a second to think. I can't make any mistakes here. Mom and Mere's future hinges on me keeping myself safe as well.

He swats at a piece of newspaper swishing past our heads. The wind continues to strengthen. We won't be able to stay upright out here in the middle of the road much longer. We need shelter, and fast.

"Look at me," he says, waiting for me to meet his eyes. "Breathe. Listen. That's gotta come out."

I'm listening. I can agree with him on the heading north toward the fire department part of his plan. But the ripping the metal out of my already bloody shoulder part, I'm not so sure I can handle.

"We can't bandage it like that. It needs pressure to stop the bleeding. Plus . . . if it shifts, it could cause more damage." He grips my good shoulder with one hand. His other hand hovers near the ruined one.

I squeeze my eyes shut and lower my head, too exhausted to argue. Then a rip of pain tears through every fiber of my being. Muscles I didn't know I had around my stomach tighten. Some sort of primal snarl erupts from my guts and shreds the night. Curse him for yanking it out without warning me.

Obviously alarmed by my fury, he freezes. The pain constricts my lungs. I close my eyes again, trying to catch my breath. Then his strong hands clamp down on my injured shoulder. The deep pressure dulls the pain a bit.

He presses his forehead to mine. "Sophie, breathe." His words ebb and flow with the pressure he applies to my shoulder.

Closing my eyes, I exhale, then rock my upper body back and forth, back and forth, and try to block out the pain as he rips at his shirt with his free hand. Seconds later, he laces a piece of cloth under my armpit and over my shoulder.

"Breathe. Breathe. Breathe," he chants. As he fumbles around the wound, the cord I used to hang Mere's compass around my neck tangles in his fingers. He gently lifts it over my head.

"I think . . . I'm . . ." I whisper, my voice hoarse as he slides the compass into a pj pocket.

"Good job, Soph." He clamps down a little harder on my shoulder.

Despite the pain, despite the howling wind, despite the flying debris, something in my chest cracks or loosens. I can't be sure which. No one has called me *Soph* since before the accident.

No one has called me *Soph* since Dad left.

CHAPTER FIFTEEN

Half the night I waste in sighs.

ALFRED, LORD TENNYSON

When we finally reach the volunteer fire department, it's deserted, locked up tight. A metal pulley clangs a warning against the vacated flagpole. I should've gone with my gut—should've known the firefighters would have moved farther south to the more populated areas where they could be of more assistance. I don't have enough energy to be disappointed. I just want to sit down somewhere—anywhere. But there's nowhere to sit, and Finn just keeps walking.

He holds a massive trash can lid in front of us to deflect whatever the gale-force winds might throw at us next. If I weren't so exhausted, I might laugh. I mean, he's protecting me from flying debris with a trash can lid. It must be hard to play the chivalrous knight with such an awful shield. But he presses forward anyway.

All the houses up here are on the beach side of the road. They're bigger than the cottage we left behind. They're sturdier, but they're no safer from the encroaching storm surge. The middle of the road is looking like a pretty comfy spot to sit when Finn points to a driveway on the left.

Left is good. Left is inland. Left is farther from the rising tide.

A driveway disappears through a tangle of scrub brush near the mailbox. The small trees and low bushes lining the way bend at ninety-degree angles. The vengeful storm smashes them against the sandy ground like grassy pancakes.

"Should we try it?" he screams at me over his shoulder.

I nod, too weak to answer. We trudge up the driveway. When we break through the trees, we see not one but two buildings perched on top of the dunes. Of course, I can't make out any of the details, but two shadows are punctuating the dark horizon, and I see no creepy flickering lights. Maybe this is one of those expensive homes with its own guest cottage.

I should be happy the driveway's so steep. It means high elevation and protection from the storm surge. It also means more work, more climbing, and more energy. I'll never make it if I don't sit down for a second.

"Finn!" I try to scream, but the strong wind squashes my weak voice.

He tromps forward without acknowledging me. I should follow, but I can't resist the temptation of the massive driftwood at the edge of the driveway. Easing myself down to the log, I baby my bad shoulder, careful not to jostle it.

The compass slips from my pocket to the ground. I rest my foot on its cord so it won't blow away. I'll grab it in a second. I just need to sit still—to not move anything for a minute. I clamp my teeth together and try to silence their chattering.

The one good thing about the icy rain is it numbs the pain in my shoulder. It kind of numbs my thoughts too. Maybe I'll just sit out the storm here. Careful to avoid any sudden movements that might reignite the pain, I half slouch, half lean against a twisted arm of driftwood rising from the main trunk. I'm starting to think my plan is so basic, it might work.

Then my comical knight in shining armor with his improvised shield realizes I'm not with him and comes back determined to rescue me.

"Come on. We're almost there." He grabs my hand.

I shake my head, praying he'll leave me alone. "I just need to sit a minute. You go ahead."

"No." He tugs me to my feet. "I'm not going anywhere without you. We're in this together."

I want to argue. We're not in this together. I can take care of myself, but I don't have the energy to disagree.

He wraps an arm around my waist. "I'll carry you if I have to."

Based on the way he's been protecting his own injured ribs, I'm pretty sure he's bluffing. The thought of me slung over his shoulder with my butt in his face is an embarrassing enough mental image that I dig deep and fan the dying embers of my determination. "No. I can do it."

Somehow, we make it up the hill together, leaning into the wind and each other. Finn aims for the big house, but I steer us toward the smaller building on the left. It's kind of protected by the larger building in front of it, and we need all the protection we can get. Up here, we're totally safe from the storm surge, but the wind gusts are even stronger. The sound morphs from the roaring freight train I've grown accustomed to into a thunderous buzz, like something out of a science fiction movie. I clamp my hands over my ears to block out the disorienting sound. I want to sit down and curl up in the duck-and-cover position we practice at school during severe weather drills. But we're so close.

Finn rattles the door. Of course, it's locked. Unlike me back at the cottage, Finn doesn't hesitate to break the small, uncovered window on the door. Careful to avoid the jagged glass, he slips his hand through the opening, finds the knob, and opens the door. Once inside, I stagger toward a sectional sofa in the center of what appears to be an open kitchen and living area. Finn shines the light around the almost bare interior, and I decide some single guy must live here, because there are zero decorations and the TV is obnoxiously large. Luckily, the larger windows have been boarded up really well, and—thank God—there's a very masculine pile of firewood stacked beside what appears to be a working fireplace.

Finn leans against the closed door as I slump on the couch, trying to catch my breath. Hugging myself, I vow to get up in a minute. I just need to close my eyes and breathe. The throbbing in my shoulder should subside if I lie perfectly still. I hear Finn exploring the house, and once in a while a drawer opens and closes.

I try to calculate how many hours of this horror we have left. The few times I've ridden out storms at home, the worst never lasted more than twelve to twenty-four hours. The storm surge might be dangerous for a few days. We might be without power and water longer than that, but the winds should die down drastically by this time tomorrow.

We'll make it. People can survive anything for thirty-six hours, right? I mean, I've seen mares laboring to deliver their foals for two days.

I'm tough.

I can handle this.

I can.

I keep my eyes squeezed shut as Finn clanks around at the fireplace. A match strikes. The familiar sound of kindling crackling and popping punctuates the deafening buzz of the wind. Heat caresses my cheek, like Dad's hands when I was little.

I focus on breathing, and not moving, and not thinking about anything—just clearing my mind and breathing. When a warm hand wiggles mine, I jump. I was so focused on myself, I kind of lost track of Finn and his bumbling around the house.

"I'm so tired. What time is it?" I groan and blink, trying to clear the cobwebs from my aching head. Clearly, I need to stick to silence and stillness.

"It's late—the middle of the night, I think. You've been lying here awhile."

Reaching for the back of the couch, I wrestle myself to a half-seated position when the realization that I've lost Mere's compass hits me.

He places a firm hand on top of mine on the cushion. "Are you okay?"

I shake my head, unable to speak.

"Where does it hurt? What's wrong?" he asks.

I try to swing my legs off the side of the couch, but they barely move. "The compass. I lost the compass."

He shoulders relax. "I'll find the compass. We need to get you in some dry clothes first and clean your shoulder." Finn sits beside me on the couch, his hip pressing against mine, his face illuminated by the fire.

His *we* brings me to attention like a double shot of espresso.

We might be stranded together in this storm. *We* might even share a Twinkie and story time. But *we* are not changing my clothes or cleaning my shoulder. I'm learning to tolerate Finn Sanders, but I'm not ready to do anything more than that.

"I'm fine. I can—" Pain rips through my shoulder when I try to sit up. My throat burns. Hurricane winds are usually cold, but this place feels like the arctic.

"You took care of me earlier. It's my turn to take care of you."

No, sir. Not happening.

When his hand brushes my arm, his eyes widen. He lifts my hand a little, pressing it to his cheek, then rests his free hand on my forehead. His already wide eyes threaten to pop from his skull.

"Crap. You're freezing." He brushes matted hair off my cold cheek.

"It's the storm and this house," I say, praying his eyeballs don't fall into my lap.

"It's not the house or the storm. Were you feeling sick earlier?"

I shake my head, too tired to argue.

He rakes his fingers through his hair, then grabs a pillow and a cushion from the far end of the huge couch. "Maybe you've lost too much blood. We need to elevate your feet. And we need to make sure you stay hydrated and warm."

When he scurries away, I assume it's for blankets and something to drink.

Trying to stay warm like he said, I wedge my hands into my armpits. Fresh blood rushes down my chest. It's warm. That's for sure. Even in the dim light, the angry red fluid stains the Crab Shack T-shirt, making the old stains pale pink by comparison.

He reappears, blanket in hand, smiling encouragingly until his eyes drop from my face to the seeping stain on my shirt.

"Holy crap, Sophie! You're still bleeding."

"Yeah." The room spins, and I close my eyes. He shuffles around the couch. When he bumps into something, he curses under his breath. I'm too exhausted to care. A second later, he's kneeling on the floor beside me, reaching through the neck of my shirt and pressing a dark towel to my wound. I don't know if it's the blood loss or just the exhaustion from fighting the storm, but even with Finn so close, I can't seem to bring his face into focus. I squeeze my eyes shut to block out the fuzziness of the world around me.

He continues applying pressure to my shoulder as I continue breathing and squeezing my eyes shut. Finally, he gets up and bangs around the kitchen. The house moans and groans around us like it's fighting to stay upright. Every once in a while, a gunshot-like pierce of wood snapping punctuates the night.

We can't win. Up here, we're sitting ducks, waiting for the next gust of wind to blow us to smithereens. Gritting my teeth, I push myself a few inches higher on the couch pillows and try to survey the house for any noticeable damage.

As I peer around the shadowy room, Finn's bare feet shuffle across the wood floor. Our eyes meet when he steps in front of the fire. I try to smile but can't. The pain in my shoulder locks the muscles in my face. My stomach tightens at the sight of the bottles clutched against his chest. One of them looks like the Jack Daniels Dad grew so fond of before he jumped ship. I can't be certain, but it looks like he's also got honey and lemon juice and God only knows what else.

The last thing I want to do now is have some kind of pitiful hurricane party.

Scratch that. The last thing I want to do is become my father.

CHAPTER SIXTEEN

I found Him in the
shining of the stars.

ALFRED, LORD TENNYSON

Finn peers down at me on the couch, his perceptive gaze on my face raising the temperature of my chilly cheeks several degrees. When I tell him I don't drink, he bursts out laughing.

"You seriously think I'm trying to get you drunk? In a hurricane? When you're sick?" He sets bottles and a pair of scissors on the coffee table, then settles beside me on the edge of the couch. His mouth is smiling, but the skin between his brows pinches together.

If I didn't know better, I'd think I hurt his feelings. "Maybe. Everybody says you'll do anything."

"Like what?"

"Like surf in a hurricane," I say pointedly. "And if you'll do that, you'll do . . ."

"Do what?" he asks as he plucks the whiskey bottle from the table and uncaps it.

"Just about anything . . . and . . ." Squirming, I hope he

133

doesn't ask why I've been listening to what people have been saying about him or why I would be interested. If the tips of my ears burn any hotter, they might warm my body and the entire room. I curl my toes into the couch cushions, wishing I could disappear, or at least create space between the two of us.

"We're not drinking this." He holds the whiskey up to my face. "It's for your shoulder. I think I got the bleeding stopped for good, but I couldn't find any first aid supplies or Tylenol."

"Oh," I say, sounding as awkward as I feel.

With his free hand, he plucks the scissors off the table and extends them to the collar of my shirt.

Wincing, I swat his hand away from my collarbone. "I can do it myself."

"You sure about that?" he asks, placing the scissors back on the table.

"I'm positive. Just help me up."

He sits frozen in place, mouth open a little, as if I've insulted him or surprised him. Tilting his head, he studies my face. "I can't believe it. You don't trust me, do you?"

Uhhh, maybe. Maybe not.

"I didn't say that."

"You don't have to. Your face did."

"Just help me to the bathroom. I'll do what you say." I gesture at the supplies on the table.

He holds my elbow as I hoist myself to my feet, then guides me to a cramped bathroom at the back of the dark house. The room spins as I lower myself to the icy toilet seat. If the living room was arctic, the bathroom is a freaking tundra. I try to keep from shivering as he heads back to the living room. When he returns a minute later, he lines the bottles on the counter beside me, then waits for me to meet his eyes.

"This is what I want you to do. Rinse your shoulder with the whiskey—gently. We don't want any more bleeding. The whiskey's not as good as rubbing alcohol or peroxide, but it's better than dirty water or nothing. Then squeeze lemon juice on the wound. It will burn, but the acid in the lemon will kill some of the tougher germs."

"We're not marinating a steak," I argue, careful not to move too suddenly.

"No. It's more like dressing a turkey." He pauses, smirking, clearly impressed with his little play on words. If my shoulder didn't hurt so badly, I might have a comeback, but I'm too exhausted to argue.

"What's the honey for?" I ask, concentrating on one spot on the floor so the room won't tilt or spin.

"Honey has natural antibiotic properties."

"How do you know all this stuff?" I stall, waiting for him to leave the room. I'm not taking off my shirt until he's on the other side of a closed door.

"Mom and I spent as much time searching for homeopathic remedies and miracle cures as we did sitting in doctors' office waiting rooms. I told you we accepted Dad's death, and it was peaceful. But that doesn't mean we just gave up as soon as he was diagnosed. We would have done anything to keep him alive. But when the suffering set in, we loved him too much . . ."

"I see," I say, pushing myself to my feet and clutching the edge of the counter with my cold fingers. I'm not so sure I do see. But I don't want to be rude, and if I don't do what he says fast, I might pass out. "Okay. Jack Daniels, lemon, honey. Got it."

He leaves his flashlight on the counter, then backs out of the room, pulling the door closed behind him. I exhale slowly then look in the medicine cabinet, but it's empty. No pain reliever. When I swing its door closed, my reflection in the mirror looks like something out of a horror film. The beam of the flashlight illuminates the bottom half of my pale face. The top half is camouflaged by shadows. My normally light brown hair hangs like dark curtains down either side of my pale face. My eyes sink into my skull zombie style.

Holding my breath, I attempt to wiggle free of my shirt. A wave of pain washes over me as the tight space closes in even further. Despite the discomfort, I refuse to cut this shirt before I know there's a replacement somewhere in this house. I wait for the room to stop spinning before I grit my teeth and yank the sleeve away from my injured shoulder. My fingers snag in the armhole, stopping the momentum of my arm, causing my shoulder to jam. I wince and watch as the floor rises to swallow my face. There's nothing I can do but wait for the impact and pray I don't further injure myself.

Snagging the edge of the counter on my descent, I lessen the severity of my collision with the floor, but probably not enough to completely hide the sound from Finn. Sure enough, seconds later, he's lifting me and cradling me against his chest. I unsuccessfully will myself to shake off the wooziness, but the thumping of his heart hypnotizes me.

At some point, the mental fog lifts, and I peer at my surroundings through one slitted eye. The fire to my right flickers and cracks, the wavering light casting ghostly fingers on the stone hearth. I'm back on the couch. It takes all my strength to glance around the room in search of Finn. He's nowhere to be found, but a smile tugs at the corners of my mouth when I spy Mere's compass propped up on the mantel.

How in the world? He found it, which means he's been outside.

Then I notice something else. I'm not wearing a T-shirt. I'm wearing a man's flannel shirt. Squeezing my eyes shut, I shiver. Sweet Jesus, he . . . he . . . changed my shirt. Maybe I should just close my eyes and die right now.

I try.

It doesn't work.

"Finn?" I call for him, but the house is eerily silent. I have no idea how long I was asleep, but I'm pretty certain not long enough to have skirted the hurricane. We must be in the eye of the storm. But where's Finn? Why would he leave me now?

If he's outside, he could get hurt. If he gets hurt, I'm alone. So much for his whole *we're in this together* motto. I steel myself for an inevitable stab of pain as I push, pull, and wiggle my way to a seated position in the corner of the couch. There is pain, but instead of the ripping and stabbing I expect, it's more pressure and bruising.

His home remedy might not be a modern-day miracle or prescription pain meds, but it's something. I definitely feel less achy, and the pain in my shoulder has lessened a bit.

Finn is taking good care of me. I could almost do more than tolerate him. I could almost . . . like him again. But that's ridiculous. I mean, maybe we could be friends here, in the isolated world of this storm, where it's just the two of us. But in the outside world, we have nothing in common, and my life is too complicated now for anything resembling romance.

This storm has thrown us together, that's all. And that's how I want it to stay. I certainly don't want to be stranded on my own. "Finn," I call, louder this time.

There's still no answer, so I drag myself to the front door. The shutters have protected us, but they also keep me blind to the rest of the world. As I pull open the door, a gust of air whips my hair. The wind may have weakened in the eye of the storm, but it's still blowing. Thankfully, it seems to have given up on the whistling and screaming. I squint into the night, pleased my eyes work better than I would have expected in the murky darkness. If nothing else, this stupid storm is teaching me to appreciate the wonders of the human body—of my human body. I had no idea I could see this well at night.

The full moon helps a bit. It's not shining like it normally would on a clear fall night, but it seems to be trying to break through a layer of clouds stretched like thin cotton balls. Movement in front of the other, larger building catches my eye. I blink, positive my eyes are playing tricks on me.

First, a pointed spire tops what I thought was the main house to our guest cottage. I blink again, and my fuzzy brain clears. It's not a spire. It's a steeple, a white church steeple rising toward the outline of a golden moon.

I thought I knew this part of the beach so well, but I had no idea this little church was tucked behind the tangled trees near the road. Something flaps in front of the church, distracting me from my surprise. No bird with an ounce of avian intelligence would be out in this hurricane, unless it were sick or injured. Plus, it's way too large for a bird. It's some sort of black material flapping in the wind—a flag maybe. No. I zero in on the movement at the front of the church.

Beyond the wide double doors of the main building is a weathered deck. The building and deck perch on a rise of sand. What appears to be some sort of railing made from twisted pickets of driftwood and maritime forest separate the deck from what must be a steep drop-off in front. From there, you would probably have a bird's-eye view of the Atlantic.

It's an eerily beautiful scene, like something out of one of the gothic romances Mom used to read before she quit romance—before Dad bolted. The black flapping draws my attention again, distracting me from the ironic loveliness of the white church outlined against the backdrop of the storm-swept barrier islands.

The wind spreads the material. My chest tightens. It's not a flag. It has arms. Strong, straight, graceful surfer's arms. It's Finn in a black windbreaker, arms stretched wide, head thrown back. He's standing atop a rickety railing in the eye of a hurricane doing his thing. What was it he said back at the first cottage? Something about sucking every last drop of life out of life.

A corner of the moon peeks through a slit in the clouds, like some prophetic spotlight shining on his face—his smiling face. He doesn't just smile. He beams, basking in the moment. I can't even remember what that kind of joy, or freedom, feels like. The closest thing I can think of is riding bareback on the beach at sunrise by myself with nothing but the pounding of hooves and waves for company, and I haven't done that in a long time.

My stomach twists when I realize Finn has something I

want. Something I don't have, or at least haven't had since I was much younger—contentment. He accepts whatever life throws at him. No, he doesn't just accept it. He embraces it. And he looks a heck of a lot happier than me or anyone else I know.

I quietly close the door and retreat to the couch, my ego as bruised as my shoulder.

Is it possible Finn knows more about life than I do? More about living than I do? Have I been doing this all wrong? Wind gusts in the chimney. A dying ember crackles to life as I ease back against the couch cushions, careful not to reopen the wound on my shoulder. I glance at the fire, avoiding the compass staring down at me from the mantel.

Finn won't be as easy to avoid when he returns.

CHAPTER SEVENTEEN

And our spirits rushed together at the touching of the lips.

ALFRED, LORD TENNYSON

A little while later, footsteps sound on the deck outside the door. I hunch down on the couch fake sleeping, not yet prepared to talk to Finn, much less look into his face—the beautiful face I witnessed outside in the storm.

The door creaks open. After it clicks shut, it sounds like Finn's taking off his jacket and flip-flops. A second later, footsteps pad toward the couch. I concentrate on the rhythmic breath of my pretend sleep. I wish he'd just go away. I need time to think.

But. No.

Of course not.

What does he do?

He moseys right over to my couch, lifts my feet, and plops down with my feet in his lap.

And I can't do a thing about it because I'm supposed to be *sound asleep.* Ugh.

So I just lie there, trying not to wiggle the feet in his lap.

His lap. His lap. Augh. My feet don't know what to do. I don't know what to do. I have no experience with boys. I mean, I don't think the slobbery, braces-clicking kisses with Pete Jones in eighth grade count. That experience didn't exactly inspire a wave of hormonal boy craziness. Then Dad and Mere wrecked. Dad disintegrated, and boys weren't a very high priority.

Now I realize how completely inexperienced and clumsy I am with the opposite sex.

Dear God, I'm going to die. Die.

Not from an injured shoulder.

Not from a horrific hurricane.

From . . . awkwardness.

The fire pops, and I jump.

"Soph?" Finn wiggles my feet—the feet resting awkwardly in his lap.

I almost laugh out loud. God must have a sense of humor, or he wouldn't have dropped me in this storm with this boy. Put me in AP Spanish, I'm your girl. AP English, I can write an analysis essay to knock your socks off. Biology, horses, you name it. I've got it covered. Heck, toss me a Rubik's Cube or challenge me in a game of speed chess. I'll take your challenge. Put me on a couch in the dark—with one Y chromosome— and I wilt like a Christmas poinsettia in July.

"Soph?" he asks again.

He can see my open eyes. I have to say something. "Yeah." Wow, Mr. Richards would be impressed by the complexity of my diction.

"How you feeling?" He squeezes my foot.

"Um—a little better, actually."

"Jack Daniels is an amazing thing." He laughs, gently lifting my feet out of his lap. He steps toward the hearth and throws another log on the fire. My jaw unclenches. My toes uncurl. I think I might survive.

"We're in the eye of the storm," he says.

"Yeah." *I kind of, sort of know this, because I've been spying on you and fake sleeping for a while now.*

"The sun will be up soon. There's something I want you to see."

"Okay."

"It's outside."

Without asking, I know beyond a shadow of a doubt what he's up to. He wants me to stand on that rickety railing.

Some deceitful, backstabbing voice that doesn't belong to me whispers something to the effect of *what's so wrong with that?*

Dang it. "Okay." I must have lost my mind.

"You mean it?" When he turns to face me, one eye narrows—like he's waiting for a *but*.

"I said okay."

He smiles. "You're going to love this. I promise."

I kind of doubt it. But I'm stuck now.

He leans down, cupping my elbow in his hand. "Oh, wait. I found something else you're going to like." He scurries off to the kitchen. When he returns, he holds something behind his back.

"More Twinkies?" I ask, expecting some disgusting excuse for food.

"Better."

Better than Twinkies.

"You're a very lucky girl." He holds out two pill bottles. "Advil *and* Tylenol."

"Where did you find them?" When I was in the bathroom, the medicine cabinet was completely empty.

"I might have borrowed them from a neighbor." He pops the cap off the Tylenol. "Now, don't get me wrong. I prefer homeopathic remedies, but when something hurts, it hurts."

"You broke into another house?" I watch as he counts out a few pills, then offers them to me. I accept, our fingers brushing as he reaches for a glass of water on the coffee table.

"I didn't take anything else. Trust me."

The boy is wearing me down. Trust him? I'm not as sure about that. But I am getting tired of arguing with him.

"Now, come on," he says. "We're going outside."

He brings me my tennis shoes and a yellow raincoat. I swallow the nausea rising in my throat along with the pills. I shouldn't have said yes. But I did. I really have lost my mind.

I slide into my shoes and push myself to standing.

Finn keeps a tight grip on the door when he opens it so it doesn't smack us in the face. Wind lifts my hair as we step outside and into the eye of the storm. He must be right about the time. The sky is dark, but it's more charcoal than black. We survived the storm's approach in the first cottage. We've almost survived its impact and another night together here in this house. This storm can't last much longer.

With the overcast skies, we might not witness the sun cresting the horizon this morning, but it will rise nevertheless. In the fading darkness, I can make out the gnarled trees at the bottom of the hill.

Sure enough, Finn leads me to the front of the church and the spindly railing. He pats the rail. "You can see forever from up here."

"You want—" My voice cracks. "You want me to stand on top of that?"

"Yes. I know you prefer to play it safe." He's challenging me. "But this is worth it. Trust me." He keeps saying that— *trust me.* "Have I ever given you a reason not to trust me?"

"Well . . ." He did blow me off for homecoming without so much as a *sorry* and doesn't seem to remember or care about it.

"Have I?" He does things I would never do—breaks into houses without a care in the world, explores the world around him in the eye of a storm, surfs in the face of oncoming hurricanes. But he also delivered supplies to a relative in need, saved Mere's compass, and cared for me when I needed him. This situation is morphing into a whole lot of confusing.

But here I am lifting my leg to the top of the railing, very ungracefully I might add, and standing on the shaky contraption. But I can't be certain whether it's the railing that's shaking or my legs. Something is trembling enough to rattle my teeth, though. Finn grips my legs around my knees. His fingers feel terrifying and tender all at the same time. I want to tell him to let go, that I've got this, but I don't. I can't stand up here alone.

I open one eye a sliver, biting down on my lower lip and bracing for the plummet to my death. Instead, I exhale. He's right. The scenery is beautiful, like an Ansel Adams photograph. Strokes of ash paint the sky. Ebony ink colors the sea. Pearly waves crash on aged-ivory sand. I never knew something so devoid of color could be so beautiful.

I drink in the pre-dawn beauty with Finn. The wind brushes my cheeks like stiff feathers. The sea oats flap, the ocean churns, the world rushes around us. Nature scuttles in a million different directions but in perfect harmony, like a well-trained orchestra. The wind, the water, the oats bend and roll and sway in rhythm.

Then a frantic, out-of-sync movement catches my eye. Careful not to move my lower body, I tilt my head, peering into the darkness down near the beach. The angry ocean has already devoured the first row of dunes. But farther back, tangled in what appears to be one of those silt fences used to protect the receding dunes, is a struggling animal—a large, struggling animal.

"Finn?"

He doesn't hear me. "Finn?" I reach behind me for his hand. When I glance over my shoulder, he looks up at me, eyebrows raised.

"There's something out there on the dunes."

"Huh?" he asks as he helps me down to the deck. "What is it?"

I open my mouth to speak, but my voice hangs in my throat. He grips both my shoulders. "What is it, Sophie?"

I wave a hand near my face as if that will somehow help me swallow or jump-start my voice or both. He steadies his eyes on my face and waits.

"It's . . . it's a horse. One of the wild ponies is trapped out there on the dunes." I grab his hand, then pull him toward the stairs leading down to the boardwalk that intersects with the main road below. "We have to do something."

"I don't see how—"

"I don't either. But it's there. Maybe it swam around the fence or maybe there's a break somewhere. I don't know. Maybe it jumped a fence."

He stares at me skeptically.

I yank him toward the boardwalk. "We have to do something," I say again.

He leans back, digging his flip-flops in and not moving. "I'm not sure. That surf is dangerous even for me," he shouts over the wind.

"Really?" My heart races. "This is the *one* time you're going to play it safe? I can't believe it. When there's an actual reason to take a risk, you're going to pass?"

He winces as though I slapped him.

I charge down the boardwalk without a backward glance. Halfway to the road, my toe catches on a loose board. I skid across several slick boards and then across gritty sand, crashing and burning in epic style. I lie facedown for a second—afraid to move, afraid I broke something important, like an ankle. When I work up the nerve to test my limbs and joints, everything seems to be in working order. The shoulder doesn't seem any worse than it already was. As I roll to my back, Finn drops to his knees beside me.

"Are you okay?" he asks.

I nod, thankful he doesn't crack a joke about my clumsiness.

He reaches for my hand. "Back there." He gestures toward the church up the hill. "I wasn't thinking about me when I said we should wait. I was thinking about you being hurt."

I glance down at my shoulder. The home remedies mixed with the two Tylenol are doing their job, but there's still some tenderness there. I won't be ready for an intense upper-body workout anytime soon. Sudden movement still makes the world tilt a bit. But the horse's dire situation did briefly distract me from my own pain and unsteadiness.

I accept his hand, allowing him to help me to my feet. "My

shoulder is fine." I twist my face into a smile. It's kind of hard with sand gritting my teeth and lips, but I'm determined.

He brushes a lock of tangled hair off my cheek. "If we're going to save the horse, we might need to keep ourselves alive for the time being." His mouth is set in a firm line, but I'm pretty sure he's trying not to laugh at me.

He clutches my hand as we cross the deserted road and cut a trail between two widely spaced oceanfront mansions. Crashing waves overpower the wind and our senses as we near the beach. We pause at the top of a sandy hill to scan the dunes. Bits and pieces of the silt fence wind back and forth through sea oats, brush, and sand, but we see no sign of the pony.

"Which way?" I ask.

"That way." He points left, shouting over the roaring surf.

I don't move. "Are you sure?"

"No." He descends the hill.

"I think it was closer." Without hard evidence or a valid argument, I find myself hesitating. I remember how Finn's gut led us to Zeke's shack, and how his gut told him to remove the metal from my shoulder. Suddenly, I want to follow my gut. I don't know how it will work out, but Finn's gut seems to work for him. I tell myself mine can work for me as I trudge down the hill in front of him. When another, steeper hill rises in front of us, I ascend it diagonally. He tags along. We pause at the crest to survey our surroundings.

Sure enough, right where I predicted, the silt fence twists and jerks. A chestnut-brown horse lies on its side, back legs tangled in the fence, thrashing for its life. It looks like the horse I saw hunkered down in the brush back at Zeke's—the one separated from his herd.

Mom and Dad's warnings about the horses swirl in my head, bringing a bit of doubt. When I was a child, my family spent thousands of hours researching, observing, and fighting to protect these animals. When other families went to the movies or bowling, we visited Eastern North Carolina libraries to find tidbits of information on these horses, which could be traced back five hundred years to the Spanish explorers who brought them here.

If my parents told me once, they told me a thousand times, *Sophie, these are not pets like our horses. These are wild animals. They need to be respected and treated as such—for their safety and for ours.* Even domesticated horses can be dangerous. A kick to the head or chest can cause permanent damage, even death. The widow of the guy who used to shoe our horses can vouch for that. An eight- to twelve-hundred-pound horse can wield a powerful kick.

As we approach, the horse's nostrils flare. He smells us. Even from this distance, the red flesh lining the insides of his nose and the whites of his wild eyes are visible. His ears flick back and forth, trying to get a read on us.

"Sophie. Wait." Finn grabs my arm, pulling me to a stop several yards from the fence. "Let's think about this a minute."

I point over his shoulder. "We don't have a minute."

In the gray pre-dawn light, angry clouds swirl to the south. Our window of calm will slam shut soon. The backside of this storm is preparing to drop on us like a sledgehammer. We can't be caught out in the open. That didn't work so well for me or my shoulder last time. Now we don't even have Finn's puny trash can lid for armor.

"We need to cut him loose," I say, raising my voice over the pounding surf and rising wind.

"Cut?" His face screws up like I'm speaking a different language. "We don't have a knife. We're going to have to get close and yank."

Clearly, he knows nothing about horses. Dealing with a panicked, wild horse's back legs is a death wish.

"I have an idea," I tell him.

"It better be good," he says, stepping aside.

The horse lifts his head from the sand, snorting and wild-eyed. I can't explain it, but as we lock eyes, I can read his mind, or at least his terror—that threatened, out-of-control, under-attack terror that constricts the chest and squeezes the air from your lungs. My palms sweat for him. I'm pretty sure I'm panting. This whole situation is beyond awful.

But it's not just the horse or the storm. It's the way everything seems to go in my life. Sisters shouldn't suffer brain injuries. Dads shouldn't choose Jim Beam over flesh-and-blood daughters. Okay, maybe human beings are a train wreck. As much as I hate to admit it, maybe we do deserve a bit of the suffering we create. But not animals—not innocent animals. This beautiful horse never did anything to anyone. And if he dies, there won't be any of Finn's peaceful beauty here. We don't even have drugs to put him out of his misery. If he dies, it's going to be slow and painful and terrifying, cut off from his herd and confused, chewed up and swallowed by the ravenous surf.

As if to prove my point, the horse shrieks. His sides heave as he tries to drag himself to his feet. With his front legs curled under his chest, he manages to heft his heavy front end a few inches above the sand. When he tries to pull his hind legs under his belly, for leverage, the silt fence cuts into his skin. Blood oozes from the leg where the fence pinches his flesh.

A rush of adrenaline shoots through my arms and legs, and instinct kicks in. I know what we have to do. I've seen Doc Wiggins do it with sick and panicked horses. One of us has to get control of the big guy's head. If we control the head, we control the rest of him. The other needs to do the untangling.

"It's now or never." Finn takes a step forward.

"Wait." I reach for his arm, but he slips away. "I know what I'm doing, Finn." I can't let him rush in headlong. I have to take the lead here. But I'd rather not risk my life. Mom needs me. Another accident would kill her—if not physically, then emotionally. And Mere needs her. If Mom loses it, there's no one to care for Mere. I vowed to take care of them both, and I will.

But this horse is a lot like Mere. He needs someone who can problem solve for him. I have to do something.

Before I can stop Finn, he steps within reach of the horse's back hooves. With the strength that comes only from adrenaline and panic, the horse manages to kick despite the fence tangling his legs. A sharp hoof grazes Finn's side. His mouth opens in a silent scream as he doubles at the waist and retreats to where I stand.

I grip his upper arm with one hand and run the other down his side, feeling for protruding ribs.

"I . . . I'm . . . fine. It just scared me." He shakes his shaggy hair out of his eyes and presses his lips together. "I'm just not sure how we're going to do this."

He looks defeated, which is such a foreign look on him, it kind of scares me.

"I told you I've got this," I say. "I've seen my vet deal with horses like this."

His face hardens a bit. "Sophie, I told you—"

"Just give me your windbreaker."

He looks doubtful, but he does what I ask. As he's slipping out of his jacket, I bend down and remove a lace from one of my tennis shoes. His eyebrows lift.

I step close to him, tilting my face up to his so I don't have to shout and further frighten the horse. "Horses are stimulated by their vision. I'm going to cover his eyes and ears with this." I hold up the jacket.

"What about that?" He points at the shoelace.

"Trust me." I toss his words back at him. After a short pause, he laughs, deep and true from his belly, then steps back to watch as I inch toward the horse's head.

"It's okay, buddy. It's okay, buddy. I got you. I got you," I chant rhythmically. He lifts his head to struggle, but the fight's gone from him. Holding my breath, I crouch behind his head for half a second. Then in one swift movement, I drape the jacket over his ears and eyes, just like I've seen Doc do. My reflexes kick in, like they always do when I'm confronted with an animal in crisis. Without pausing to think, I gently swing one thigh over the horse's neck, straddling him. Breathing deeply, I tighten the jacket around the top half of his head.

Glancing over my shoulder at Finn, I flash a thumbs-up. With my free hand, I wrap the shoelace around the horse's top lip. But I need more leverage to create the makeshift twitch Dad showed me how to use. The calming distraction works on our horses when they're spooked. I hope it will work on the wild pony too.

"Help. Please," I hiss, lifting my jaw toward Finn and handing him the shoelace. The horse's neck tenses between my thighs. One wrong move and one or both of us could be bitten, kicked, or crushed. "Loop it. Twirl it tight and hand it back to me."

Our eyes lock for a fraction of a second. He passes me the twisted lace without question. When I tilt my head toward the horse's muscular hind end, Finn nods and steps toward the horse's back legs. Sheets of muscle ripple beneath my thighs, but the horse's shrouded head remains flat on the sand. I loop the lace around his top lip, tight enough to make him think about it, but not tight enough to hurt. His jaw spasms, and the lace slips through my slick palm. We're pressing our luck here. This situation has the potential to get really ugly, really quickly.

I don't have to tell Finn to approach from a different angle this time. He's a quick learner. There's no way to completely avoid the horse's back legs, but he gets a somewhat safer angle by approaching the horse from above instead of from directly behind. I focus on immobilizing the horse's head and neck as Finn reaches toward the silt fence and the thrashing legs. Gritting my teeth, I squeeze my eyes shut, refusing to be dislodged as the horse squirms beneath me.

I count to one hundred to maintain my calm focus. When a hand clamps my good shoulder, I startle. Of course, it's Finn. He's grinning ear to ear. He nods at the horse's back legs. Blinking, I exhale. We did it. The horse is untangled—free.

"Stand back," I say, releasing the twisted shoelace and dismounting the horse's neck. Sliding the windbreaker from its head, I retreat. Finn follows close behind. From the safety of the next dune, I turn to check on our horse. He's standing, but his head hangs below his withers, and he sways tiredly.

The wind picks up as I turn back to Finn. "We did it," I murmur.

Holding my gaze, he pulls me into a hug. "*You* did it," he says against my hair.

As I look up at his face, a ripple of heat passes from my cheeks, to my chest, to my belly, where it settles and spreads to the rest of me. The world buzzes around me in a blur of white noise. This time it's not from the storm around me. It's from something inside me. My vision narrows until all I see is his face, his eyes, his . . . lips.

My breath catches, but I don't pull away. My lips part, and I don't try to stop them. He leans closer. When his lower lip brushes mine, I can taste the salt on him. My head tilts. It's kind of like riding a galloping horse. Your body just kind of knows if you want to stay on, you have to lean into it. And all of me is leaning in.

Finn's hand slides around the back of my neck. My chest rises and falls, like I'm running. My pulse pounds in my ears. I've never wanted anything so desperately in my life. It's instinctual. I couldn't stop this train if I wanted to.

A crack of lightning rips the sky.

But Mother Nature sure can.

My eyes fly open. Finn's hand drops from my neck. Without speaking, we bolt hand in hand for the safety of the church and its little parish house. We've lived through enough hurricanes to know lightning and hurricanes don't mix. At best, this is a strange development in the weather. At worst, it's the precursor to weather the likes of which the Outer Banks hasn't seen in the last century.

CHAPTER EIGHTEEN

Theirs not to reason why,
Theirs but to do and die.

ALFRED, LORD TENNYSON

T here isn't time to discuss the significance of the thunder and lightning, but by how fast Finn's running, it's pretty obvious he's thinking what I'm thinking. Hurricanes don't generally spawn lightning. It has something to do with lightning being formed by vertical winds, and the hurricanes being made up of mostly horizontal winds. When a storm like this discharges the kind of lightning we just witnessed, it signals something bizarre at work. If I were a betting girl, I'd put money on some kind of super weather event in the making.

In the two or three minutes it takes us to reach the road and the boardwalk leading up to the church, the wind increases dramatically. The hair on my arms and the back of my neck tingles from the electricity in the air. I glance over my shoulder near the top of the hill to check on our wild pony friend. My heart sinks at the sight of him swaying on three legs, his fourth tucked up like he doesn't want to put weight on it. In that condition, he won't reach the next dune. He won't escape the storm surge. He won't make it.

"This sucks," I grumble. With hands balled into fists at my sides, I rack my brain for a last-ditch rescue attempt—something brave and heroic. Maybe I could craft a halter and lead rope out of belts and clothing and coax the horse to safety with my super Spidey horse sense.

But neither of us is wearing a belt or any extra clothes. And this isn't a domesticated horse. This is a wild animal.

"It sucks big time," Finn agrees.

Despite my clenched-jaw determination, I know in my heart Mom, Dad, and Doc Wiggins would all tell me to let go and trust the animal and its instincts. I could concoct some epic rescue—like the well-meaning tourists who tried to herd an escaped horse to safety but ended up herding the panicked animal into oncoming traffic—and cause more harm than good.

Finn tugs on my hand, his face as grim as mine feels. With tears welling in my eyes, we race the last fifty yards to shelter. As we enter the house, Finn slams the door behind us. Leaning back against the door, he pants. I stumble to the couch. Resting my elbows on my knees, I grip my head in my hands. Our little sanctuary on higher ground doesn't feel so safe anymore—not with the backside of the storm bearing down on us and that poor horse out there on his own.

"Sophie, I think we might want to hole up in the closet till this passes."

I nod. The rising wind speaks for itself as I race around the living area grabbing pillows and blankets. Trying to remain calm, I remind myself we're out of reach of the storm surge. In most cases, water is more dangerous than wind. But this hurricane, with its freakish lightning, suddenly makes me doubt what I know to be true—that and the tension of the air. I swear I can feel some sort of magnetic force pushing and pulling on the frame of the house. I don't know whether to be afraid it will splinter and scatter or afraid it will implode on us.

"This way." Finn motions to the back room I haven't explored.

I clutch the linens against my chest and follow. "Do you think—"

"We're going to be fine. I know," he says. But the crease between his eyebrows is deep. He grunts as he chucks clothes and shoes out of the closet to make room inside for the two of us. We work in silence, lining the floor with pillows and blankets. When a gust of wind rattles the bedroom windows, Finn pulls me inside the cramped space and closes the door. Our ragged breathing and the muffled wind camouflage the silence.

We sit side by side this time, with our backs pressed against the rear wall and our knees drawn to our chests. When I shiver, Finn drapes an arm across my neck, careful to avoid my injured shoulder. I lean into his side, careful to avoid his bad ribs. We're wrecks.

"We've got to quit meeting in dark closets. People will talk," he says, joking as he bumps his knee against mine.

I glance around our hiding spot. I can't see Finn's face, but I can smell him—all sticky salt and rainwater. "What time do you think it is?" I ask.

He shrugs. "Before noon. It doesn't really matter. Does it?"

"Do you think it will last much longer?"

He shrugs again. "No idea."

I turn my face toward where his should be, inches from mine in the darkness. "You don't care about anything, do you?"

"I care about a lot of things." His breath brushes my cheek, and I know he's turned to face me as well. "I just try not to worry about stuff I can't control."

Here we go again. "I prefer to think of it as using resources wisely. I can get more done in eight hours than most people can in twelve."

"You know about *chronos* and *kairos*, right?" he asks.

"Yes, Finn. I know my Greek mythology." Seriously? Where is he going with this? He called us *friends* back at Zeke's. Anyone who knows anything about me knows I've got some mean mythology chops.

"Yeah, but I'm not talking about the gods. I'm talking about the words."

"They both mean *time*." I interrupt, trying to ward off another one of his lectures.

"Yes and no," he says. "Yes, they both mean *time*. But chronos is clock time—schedules, calendars, and alarms. Kairos is more like *moment* than *time*. It's like nirvana. It's riding the perfect wave. It's the blush of sunrise on a deserted beach. It's not keeping track of time. It's losing sight of it—being lost in the moment—in the zone."

Despite his poetic little monologue and the warmth of his body beside mine, I feel my defenses going up.

"You're saying I'm too uptight about time?" I scoot a little toward my end of the closet.

"I didn't say that."

"You didn't have to."

"But think about it. It is kind of a trade-off. If you focus on one, you lose the other. You can't have both."

I can't take it any longer. I need him to shut up, to stop all this talk of being lost in the moment. Before I can control it, my body commits the ultimate act of treachery. The upper half of me tilts forward, close enough to brush the corner of his mouth with my lips.

When he nibbles my lower lip, my insides melt. I'm pretty sure my brain melts. I lace my hands behind his neck just as he pulls back an inch.

Drawing my hands from behind his neck, he grasps them against his pounding heart. "Are you *sure* you want to do this?"

My heart snaps in my chest like a rubber band. Maybe I read his signs all wrong. "Do you?"

He lets out a breathy laugh. "Are donuts a delicacy?"

Shaking my head, I try to make sense of his confusing answer. The awkward pause lasts just long enough to clear my head.

"I'm . . . not sure what I want," I say, being totally honest.

"That's what I thought."

"You're wrong about one thing, though."

"What's that?"

"I'm not all chronos."

The laugh I'm growing dangerously fond of erupts from his belly. He squeezes my hand. "When this storm ends and we're not trapped in a closet, I want to see more of *that* Sophie."

I squeeze his hand in return, trying to picture the two of us together back in the real world—me with my schedules and responsibilities and calendars, him a free spirit going wherever the next wind or wave takes him.

"Finn?"

"Yeah?"

I want to ask him what he was thinking back in ninth grade when he didn't show up for the dance, moved away, and didn't call. But I don't want to make a big deal out of something that was obviously not a big deal to him.

"Ummm . . ." If I had a free foot, I'd kick myself in hopes of restarting my voice.

"I'm all ears here." He rests his head on the wall close to mine as though he's got all day, and I guess he does.

I say in a small voice, "I just—I've always wondered why you never got in touch or explained about standing me up. I mean, now I know about your dad . . . but still . . ."

"Standing you up?" The air between us shifts when he lifts his head away from the wall.

Surely I wasn't so unimportant that he can't even remember we were supposed to meet at the dance. I try to slide my hand out of his, but he squeezes a little tighter. "Yeah. You know. We were going to meet at the ninth-grade homecoming dance. I mean, it was our first high school dance. I was pretty excited . . ." I hate the way my voice keeps trailing off, betraying me with its weakness.

"All the teachers knew about my dad. I thought one of them would have said something to everyone."

My posture's so stiff, I'm brittle—a puff of air and I might disintegrate. I don't answer.

"They didn't tell you, did they? About my dad?" he asks, like he recognizes the hurt in my voice despite my best attempt to hide it. "It happened so fast—him being selected for the trial. But I should've told you in person. I'm so sorry, Sophie. I—"

He swallows. "That's why you've been so distant with me, isn't it? Because I didn't show up for the dance?" He sounds relieved, like he just remembered where he left his phone or keys.

My chest untightens a notch, and it hits me. I've been so worried about my hurt feelings, I've barely considered how awful it must have been to leave so suddenly under such horrible circumstances. My broken heart abruptly seems a little immature and a little overly dramatic.

When he pulls me to his side, my frayed nerves untangle a bit. "I was stupid—" I lean into the warmth of his side.

"You could never be stupid, Bookworm." He rests the side of his face on the top of my head.

I can't be certain in the pitch dark if he's smiling, but something in his voice makes it sound like he is.

If we survive this storm together, I think I may be able to find a way to give him a second chance.

CHAPTER NINETEEN

A beam in the darkness: let it grow.

ALFRED, LORD TENNYSON

We sit for what seems like a lifetime in the dark without saying a word. Finn's arm never leaves my shoulders. Despite the blackness, I occasionally feel his gaze on my face.

"Can we lie down?" he asks. "My back's killing me."

"Yeah." I try to sound cool, but I'm not sure how that's going to work. Are we going to lie face-to-face? I lick my gums and teeth in a lame attempt to freshen my breath.

"Here," he says, patting the flannel blanket on the floor as he squishes against the back wall of the closet. I lie parallel to his body like a two-by-four. When I shiver, he pulls me back against his chest, and it doesn't feel weird or awkward. It feels safe.

It's suddenly hard to believe I thought I needed to protect myself from this—from Finn. Hard to believe I thought closing my heart, keeping it safe, was more important than the warm embrace of a boy I care about—really care about.

Yesenia would be so happy. She loves being right. The swishy feeling in my stomach kind of affirms that Tennyson quotation she's always repeating. Plus, she'd finally get to add a few checks to the bucket list she's been keeping for me all these years.

When something crashes in the distance, I flinch and remind myself I have to survive this storm if I hope to check anything off Yesenia's silly list.

"I wish we had music or a book or something," I say over the racket of my pulse and racing heart.

"We could talk." His breath brushes the edge of my ear and sends tickly shivers along my throat and neck.

"About what?" I ask.

"Anything."

"How much longer do you think this will last?"

"Anything but the weather. Okay?"

"Okay." I browse my mental file cabinet but come up blank, suddenly realizing how small my world is. My life is pretty much school, school, school, the barn, and worrying about Mere and Mom and . . . school. "Um, I love to read."

"Everybody knows that. Tell me something I don't know. Greatest fear?"

Everything. I can't tell him there are too many choices to pick just one.

He squeezes my hip. "Come on, give me something here. What's your greatest fear?"

I remain frozen in place, not wanting to sever the line from his arm to his hand to my hip but not wanting to answer his question either. No. It's more than that. I don't know *how* to answer his question. "I don't know."

"Yes, you do." He jostles my hip again.

"What are you afraid of?" I whisper.

"I'm afraid of spiders and snakes and opossums."

"Opossums? No, you're not." I nudge him in the stomach with my elbow. There's no way a guy who surfs in hurricane waters can be afraid of a furry, pointy-nosed critter. He must be kidding.

"Wait. Wait." The wind howls while he thinks. "Got it—climate change."

"Really? You're afraid of climate change?"

"Yep. It's serious. If we don't do something to reverse the arctic ice melt, we'll be under water—Outer Banks, bye-bye."

"Hmm."

"What?"

"I just thought you'd be afraid of something . . . scarier."

"What's scarier than melting polar icecaps and rising sea levels?"

"For me—losing something I love." My words drape over us like a heavy quilt.

"Losing things we love is a part of life, Sophie. We can't avoid it."

"Yes, but . . ." I tell myself to stop, abort, shut up.

"But what?"

"It's not just my sister I lost in the accident. I mean . . . You know what I mean. I lost my dad too."

"Oh, Soph. I'm sorry. I didn't know he died—"

"He didn't." I force air through tight lips. "It was worse than that."

"Worse?"

I blink back the tears in my eyes. "Yes." I take a deep breath and swallow before continuing. "He didn't die. He . . . he walked out on us." I've never said this out loud to anyone. Of course,

Yesenia knows, but she respects my silence. We haven't talked about it since the week after Dad left, when she asked about his absence. I said he needed space, but Yesenia's smart. She didn't miss the increasing number of beer cans on the coffee table or the way Dad's complexion turned from golden brown to sickly yellow.

Finn squeezes me even tighter, resting his chin on top of my head. We lie in silence for several long minutes.

"It's bad to lose someone you love because of an accident or sickness. It's worse when the person makes a conscious decision to walk away and not look back." Pinching my eyes closed, I will myself not to cry.

"When did it happen?"

"It was a few months after the accident. He couldn't handle Mere's disability, the mounting medical bills, or his own guilt. He was the one driving. He started drinking and taking too many pills to deal with the pain and just never stopped."

"Would it have been better if he died?"

"No. Yes. I don't know." I bite the inside of my cheek. "It's why . . . I just can't . . . It just seems like I always lose people. I can't lose anyone else."

"I don't know—you're pretty tough." He rubs his fisted knuckles playfully in my hair, the same way Dad did when I was a kid.

I don't laugh. "No, Finn. I'm serious. I'm not like you."

The closet is quiet. For once, he doesn't have anything to say. He lets the stillness settle around us. After what seems like forever, he finally speaks. "Then I guess you better get some cats or something."

"That's a pretty good idea, actually." I laugh, trying to

sound unconcerned and trying not to think about how much I miss Jim's little whiskered face.

"You might change your mind," he mumbles a minute later, unable to disguise the exhaustion in his voice. We've been going like this for too long.

"Doubtful," I whisper, lying perfectly still, and then listening to his rhythmic breathing. I don't begrudge him the sleep. We're both drained. If we're going to think clearly, we both need rest.

But I can't sleep. I lie awake rehashing our conversation. I can say I won't open my heart to that kind of risk ever again. But the truth is I think I already have. Finn seems to have weakened my defenses and snuck inside when I wasn't looking.

like glimpses of forgotten dreams.

ALFRED, LORD TENNYSON

When I open my eyes, I feel like I've aged seventy years. My bones hurt. My muscles ache. My shoulder throbs, reminding me I should probably take some more Tylenol. But when I hear Finn's soft breathing beside me, I smile despite the discomfort.

I lift my head a couple of inches off the floor. Nothing tilts or spins. I must be improving. Cocking my ear to the door, I listen for the storm. But the house is silent. The world is silent. Sitting up, I reach around in the dark for the doorknob on the inside of the closet. The room outside the door is slightly less black than the closet around us.

Part of me wants to rest, but an image of that poor horse invades my thoughts. He probably didn't make it in his condition. My heartstrings stretch until they threaten to snap when I think about the wild horse out there alone. If he managed to survive but didn't get far, he'll need fresh water.

I hate to wake Finn, but I have to check on that horse. We also need a plan. We need a phone and probably medical attention for both of us.

"Finn, wake up." I wiggle his shoulder, ready to do something—anything. I have to let Mom know I'm okay. I'm sure she and Mere are fine. They left with time to spare. But I need to *know* they're okay, and despite my text, Mom must be going crazy by now. "I think the storm has passed."

"Umm hmm," he answers, but makes no effort to move.

"We have to get out of here and get help." I clap my hands in the general vicinity of his face when he still doesn't budge. The sharp noise brings him to attention, accomplishing what my voice couldn't.

He sits up, banging his head on the wall and grunting. "Huh? What? Oh. Right. The storm." Standing, he grips his lower leg and shakes it like it fell asleep or something.

"I think it's passed. It's quiet out there." Rubbing my sore back, I push myself to standing. "And we need to go look for that horse."

Finn hobbles around behind me, oddly quiet. We move toward the living room like wounded warriors. His shoulder pops when he stretches. Soft light filters in through the boarded-up windows, shining on the gray embers in the fireplace. As I hold my breath, we approach the front door together. Without speaking, we step across the threshold and onto the deck.

Wind blows the hair off my face, but it's more like a really brisk breeze than a gale-force wind. Tree limbs crisscross the driveway like pickup sticks. The railing at the front of the church that supported my weight yesterday leans forward precariously. One strong gust will send it tumbling down the sand. Shards of stained glass reach up from the bottom of a large round window, pointing at the disgruntled clouds churning northward.

Standing tall and straight, the church steeple remains in stark contrast to all the destruction surrounding us. The trees around the buildings have been leveled like one of Aunt Mae's pastures in the wake of her Bush Hog. Blown in from who knows where, an overturned lawn chair lies on its side. Broken glass, torn shingles, and a tattered flag litter the parking lot beside the church.

"Let's see if we have a better view from the church," Finn says without looking at me.

"Do you think it's safe?" I drag my feet, wondering if we're pushing our luck up here.

"It looks solid. Just don't get too close to the edge."

"Don't worry, I won't," I say, stepping over a stick blocking our path. Soon we're standing on the church deck, scanning the horizon, the dunes, the shoreline. There's nothing, no one—no emergency personnel cruising the road below, no Coast Guard helicopter patrolling the beach. We're on our own. That's something only coastal natives and hurricane survivors fully understand. Just because you survive the high winds and actual storm doesn't mean you're safe. Very often lives are lost *after* a storm because of flooding or injury or plain old stupidity.

We can't let our guard down. We need to be careful. But I can't stop thinking about the injured horse.

Finn seems to read my mind. "He's fine, Sophie. Those horses are like dinosaurs. They'll survive everything short of a nuclear event or a great asteroid."

"But he was alone and injured." I squint down at the dunes, but it's useless. Without the advantage of standing on the railing, I can make out only a thin sliver of sand at the ridge of the dune line.

"He didn't have to go far. Just beyond the storm surge." Finn's voice is optimistic, but his sentences are oddly short and to the point.

I chew on my lip, wondering if I've done something to offend Finn. Or said something to annoy him. Or maybe he just woke up on the wrong side of the closet; the boy hasn't cracked a joke since he woke up. It doesn't matter. We don't have time to stand around chatting anyway.

"He'll be hungry." My stomach growls in sympathy.

"You're hungry," Finn says, obviously trying to distract me from my concern and change the subject. "Under the right conditions, animals can go without food for days—maybe weeks."

I'm not going to be dissuaded so easily. "These aren't the *right* conditions. And he can't go days or weeks without water. Please—let's just look around."

He runs a hand through his hair. The *please* seems to crack his resolve. "Okay. But we need to eat and clean your shoulder before we go traipsing down to the beach. And if we can't find him quickly, he's on his own. He'll be fine."

Back in the kitchen, we scrounge around in the cabinets for something to eat. I find a box of unopened crackers and a jar of peanut butter. He finds a bottle of apple juice in the fridge and a gallon of milk. Finn was smart to leave the refrigerator door closed last night. The juice isn't cold, but it's not warm either. We agree it's fine to drink. We can't drink the milk, but I have an idea for the container.

Sitting at the small round table, we share a knife but don't talk. We should be giddy with excitement. We survived. It may take a few hours or most of the day, but we'll find help. Someone will be out looking for survivors now that the storm has passed.

Standing, I brush cracker crumbs from my lap, pour the milk down the drain, then head toward the bathroom with the empty jug.

"What're you doing?" he asks.

"Going to get water from the toilet tank in case we find the horse."

His forehead wrinkles with doubt.

"It's not ideal, but it'll work," I say, stopping to down the Advil he left on the table with the last of my juice.

I know one gallon of water isn't going to do much for a horse that size, but a little bit of something is better than a whole lot of nothing. On the way back from the bathroom, I grab Mere's compass from the mantel. There's no way I'm losing it again.

Finn sits at the kitchen table, gripping his head in his hands. He doesn't speak when I set the water and compass near him on the table or when I start digging around in the kitchen drawers.

Lifting his head, he tracks me with his eyes. "What are you looking for?"

"This." I turn around after pulling pen and paper from the drawer beside the phone.

"Are we taking notes or something?"

"No. We're *leaving* notes." I turn back to the counter and lean down to start writing. *Dear Homeowner . . .*

Finn moves up behind me. "We didn't leave a note at the other place."

"We didn't have time—" I stop when he reaches into the drawer at my hip and starts rummaging around.

"What the—" He pulls out a small cardboard box with a picture of a radio on the front. "This would have come in handy yesterday."

"It probably needs batteries," I say without looking up from my thank-you note to the person whose house we invaded.

"No. Look. It's genius." He taps the box. *"Uses rechargeable lithium-ion battery, hand crank, or solar power."* He drops the unopened box into a plastic grocery bag. "We're taking this with us."

Capping the pen, I cross my arms. "We can't take anything. The storm's passed. It was different when we didn't know if we'd survive."

"Sophie, we still don't know if we'll survive. We take the radio."

His terseness throws me off. "Okay. Whatever." I uncap the pen and write a P.S.—*hope you don't mind we borrowed the weather radio as well.*

Finn drops a handful of granola bars in the plastic bag, then shoves each arm through one of the handles, like he's wearing a makeshift backpack. He and I both reach for the milk jug on the table and bump hands.

"I can carry something." I pull the water from his grasp.

He doesn't even argue. Now I *know* something is wrong.

"Finn, are you okay?"

"Sure." His lips curve into what would be a genuine smile on anyone else. But without a sparkle in his eyes to match, he's not fooling me. When he smiles, his eyes always light up—always.

"You're never this serious—or this quiet."

"I'm good. I think this storm just knocked the wind out of me or something." He pauses before nudging my good shoulder with his free hand. "Pun intended. Get it? Knocked the *wind* out of me?"

He's trying a little too hard, but at least he seems more like himself with the goofy word play.

"Let's hit it," he says, moving toward the door and holding it open for me.

We comb the dunes without speaking. The roiling storm surge makes it too noisy to hear each other without shouting. The water rose at least five feet overnight and ripped away huge mounds of sand. The sea oats and dune where we rescued the wild horse are completely submerged.

My insides twist like a rip current. The only signs of our four-legged friend are a few smudged hoof prints.

Finn turns to face me and leans close so I can hear him. "He must've headed inland."

"Or been dragged out to sea." I peer out over the angry Atlantic.

"Why do you always have to be that way?" he barks over the waves, his jaw firm.

"What do you mean?" I ask, taking a step back.

"You always expect the worst." The words are harmless enough, but his voice sounds accusatory.

I wasn't expecting that from him, and I wasn't expecting how those five simple words could hurt like a fist to my mid-section. "I don't know." I brush the tangled hair from my face so I can see him better.

There's pain in his eyes, as though *I* hurt him.

"Finn, you're right. I'm sorry. I shouldn't be so negative. We have a lot to be thankful for. We're alive. We made it—together. I just . . . I just can't bear the thought of that poor animal, all alone . . ." My gut tells me to accept it—there's a good chance the horse didn't make it. But my heart reminds me that Finn has been right more than once. Maybe he'll be right again.

A shadow swoops over us. We glance toward the racing clouds in unison. What looks like a black-and-white cross punctuates the sky above our heads. When the black cross-pieces flap, I realize it's not a levitating religious symbol. It's a bird—a massive bird, like Pteranodon size. He glides on the brisk wind, inches above our heads. Peering at us from a beady black eye, he squawks, then rises on a current of air.

"Was that an—" Finn's mouth hangs open on his unfinished sentence.

"Ha!" I shake my fist in the air, beaming. My face stretches when I smile, really smile. "An albatross!"

"No way. They don't travel this far south." Puzzled, he squints at the gargantuan bird as it tips one wing, rocking to one side and then the other.

If I didn't know better, I'd think the bird was teasing us. "They don't *normally* travel this far south. But that's an albatross. The storm must've blown it off course or something." I track it as it glides farther and farther away.

"How do you know it's an albatross?"

"I just do. Trust me." I don't go into how Doc Wiggins is like a part of my family or how he's an avid bird-watcher. I remember the pictures of the Hawaiian nesting grounds Doc Wiggins visited two years ago. He lectured me on the birds when he returned.

"That was definitely an albatross," I say again.

"It doesn't make sense, though. The only thing less sensible would be a penguin sighting."

He's right. It doesn't make sense, and I'm really tired of things that don't make sense. I'm starting to realize life might be easier if I quit trying to make sense of everything. It's hard to believe so much has changed in two short days. It's hard to believe how much *I've* changed in two short days.

Not knowing how to deal with the dead-serious Finn in front of me, I place a playful hand on my hip, hoping for a reaction from the boy I've grown close to during this storm. "Thank you, Captain Obvious."

He cups his hand over his eyes, squinting for one last glance at the massive bird, and ignores my attempt at humor. "You know they're a good omen, right? Like good luck on steroids."

I let my hand fall to my side. "Um, have you ever read *The Rime of the Ancient Mariner?*"

"Exactly."

My jaw drops, and I prepare my argument about how wrong Finn is about this. The stupid mariner shoots the bird that leads them out of the ice jam in Antarctic waters. The guy's doomed with a capital D when the rest of the ship's crew turns on him for killing the bird. They force him to wear the massive, dead bird as some sort of symbol of regret or something. That's where the saying *an albatross around your neck* comes from. That's quite a burden to have on a ghost ship lost at sea.

But before mariner-dude killed the bird—I never could figure out why he killed it—the bird was the lucky charm that brought the wind they needed to escape the Arctic Sea. To this day, sailors believe albatross are a good omen—a symbol of land. Which is totally wrong. The birds can live at sea for years without access to land.

But suddenly, I don't want to argue. I want to hope. I want Finn to be right. I want this to be a sign from the universe—a sign that everything is going to be okay.

CHAPTER TWENTY-ONE

I slip, I slide, I gloom, I glance.

ALFRED, LORD TENNYSON

Finn finally turns away from the speck of black and white receding on the horizon. "Let's get out of here. When they allow residents back on the island, the Wild Horse Fund volunteers will be tracking the horses and checking the fence line."

He's correct, of course. One way or the other, the horse is gone. I have to focus on Mom and Mere now.

"Okay, let's go," I say, scanning the dunes again and praying for an equestrian miracle. When no natural or supernatural horses materialize, I lift my shoulders and prepare for the final chapter in my and Finn's hurricane survival story.

He stops beside a clump of sea oats and pauses for a second. His shoulders lift, like he's preparing to deliver a speech. "I kind of thought we might . . ."

"Kind of thought we might what?" I ask, glancing over my shoulder at him.

"I kind of thought we might go check for Zeke at the lighthouse before we head south. I mean, the storm was worse than any of us expected. I think we should offer to take him to the mainland with us."

Head north. Again? Away from safety. Away from Mom and Mere.

Um.

No.

"Finn, I can't. I have to get to Manteo. Now. My mom is going to be freaking out if I don't get in touch with her."

He shoves his hands in his pockets. "Fine."

He trudges up the dune in front of us, his back stiff and straight. I remind myself that Zeke is his family. Finn is probably just as worried as my mom is.

"How long do you think it will take to get to Manteo?" I ask.

"Not long."

"Really?" It must be at least fifteen miles, maybe more. On foot, with the possibility of flooding and downed power lines, it seems it would take quite some time. "How?"

"Yeah. We're going to borrow a car."

Borrow? He says it so casually, like he's going to borrow a friend's pencil in class. As we crest the last mound of sand before the level road, I look both ways for traffic. Of course, the road is desolate—not a car in sight, but there are plenty of downed branches.

"Where will we find a car to borrow?" I ask. "What about keys?"

"In a garage. If we can't find keys, I've got this." He taps his pointer finger against his temple.

"You're going to fire the engine with your brain power?" I slow down, assuming he'll stop to explain. But he presses forward.

I don't like this. Our crimes are escalating. First, it was breaking and entering for self-preservation. Then petty theft for convenience and safety. But grand theft auto sounds like something that could haunt us on our college applications and resumes.

I tell myself I would want someone to borrow my truck if it would save a life or reunite a family. Plus, we'll be careful, and it will get me to Mom and Mere faster. I have no better solution of my own, so I tag along behind him.

We backtrack to the houses we passed on our way to our church parsonage sanctuary. But Finn's optimism is misplaced. There's nothing but drifts of sand and seaweed and broken timbers in the first garage. The next three are pretty much the same except for the overturned fishing boat wedged sideways in the second. I guess these people were smart enough to evacuate all their vehicles. That's what Mom and I were trying to do.

The devastation around and between the houses is beyond depressing. The wreckage everywhere I look makes me wonder what Mom and I have to look forward to when we're finally allowed to go home. Outer Banks residents, like their horses and their ancestors, are tough and resilient, but it's going to take more than a strong will to put this mess back together. It's going to take lots and lots of money and time—months, if not years, to piece back together what a vengeful Mother Nature ripped apart.

The sky darkens, and a light mist tickles my cheeks as we head away from what appears to be the last house as far as we can see.

"Now what?" I ask, glancing at the ominous sky. The outer bands of wind and rain that follow behind a hurricane may not be as dangerous as what we've experienced, but I'm not exactly keen on enduring more severe weather.

Finn seems to read my mind. "Don't worry about the weather, Sophie."

"Me, worry?" I deadpan. Then I sigh. "It can't get any worse, I guess. You're right."

He chuckles for the first time today, and the weight in my heart eases a bit.

"My two favorite words," he says, smiling and surveying the road to the north and south. "Now I need to be right about finding us some transportation."

It doesn't look promising. "What about your car?"

"It's wrecked, Bookworm. Remember?"

"The windshield's busted, that's for sure. And it's off the side of the road. But if we could get it back on the road and not drive too fast, it might get us to Manteo?" I shrug, wanting to get this show on the road and not caring much about what kind of ride we take. Plus, it would be kind of nice to avoid felony charges and a prison stay.

"I like how you think. Let's try it," he says, grabbing my hand and leading me down the center of the road.

"How's your side?" I ask as we head south.

"Not bad. How's the shoulder?"

"Not too bad. The Tylenol helps." The medicine eases the pain in my shoulder, and something about holding his hand eases some of the pain in my heart. It feels good, normal, healthy to be physically connected to another person—a boy I like, not a family member I'm holding on to for dear life.

We walk without talking. The wind and surf drown out the need for conversation. The Blazer comes into view several minutes later. Less than forty-eight hours ago, we'd fought the wind and were delayed by my shoulder injury. When we evacuated the first cottage, it seemed like we'd hiked miles in the dark.

Now, in daylight with the wind at our backs, I realize our great retreat was maybe a mile, two miles at best. Finn breaks into a jog as we near the vehicle. I scurry to catch up.

He smacks the Blazer like an old mule. "You're one tough girl," he says. His enthusiasm dies when he gets a better angle of the front of the car. The hood's dented, the windshield smashed out.

I give him space as he peeks inside the front seat. "It's pretty nasty in there." He glances over his shoulder at me, like he expects me to complain.

"I can handle nasty if you can get it back on the road." I try not to look at the spear-like tree limb protruding from the crack in the glass. A couple of feet in either direction could have ended with one of us as a human shish kebab.

Finn yanks the driver's side door, reaches around the steering wheel, and wiggles the key in the ignition. Something clicks under the hood, and that's it. His tough old girl just sits there. Cursing under his breath, he pulls a lever under the dashboard, and the hood pops up. As he steps to the front of the car to inspect the engine, I step to the back of the Blazer to check out the cargo area. Lying on top of several boxes are a couple of beach towels. I yank the rear swinging door with the intent of grabbing the towels, but it doesn't budge.

"You need help?" Finn peeks around the raised hood.

"I've got it." I force a smile and give the handle a fierce pull.

"Bang down with your fist," he says, then ducks back under the hood.

I follow his instructions, and *the old girl* opens on the third try—just like he said she would.

Reaching for the towels, I glance up at the sky. The clouds are dark. More rain is on the way. It's going to be difficult navigating the roads with all the downed trees. I don't want to think about driving in the rain with reduced visibility and no windshield to protect us from the elements. Trying to keep my mind off Mom and Mere and the weather, I keep busy drying off the front seats with the towels.

Finn steps around the hood and toward me. "I think I've got it," he says.

"Well, start it, and let's go." I can't take another minute of standing around.

"No. You start her. I push," he says, heading to the back of the car.

I scrunch up my face, studying the precarious angle of the Blazer's back tires. I'm not an engineer, but it looks risky. It looks like if the car shifts back or to the right, anyone behind it could be trapped, maybe even crushed by the back tires.

"I don't know . . ."

"Sophie, I've done this a million times. She gets good traction. You drive. I'll push, and we'll be out of here in no time."

I want to believe him. He's done this *a million times*, and we need to get going. I take the keys when he hands them to me.

Ignoring the pain in my shoulder, I place the last dry towel on the seat and slide in behind the steering wheel. My feet swish in water pooling on the floor mat, and I notice the homeopathic book is waterlogged. An empty Doritos bag bobs in the mess. But Finn's *Don't Sweat the Small Stuff* somehow survived the crash, pressed in between the donut box and the underside of the dashboard.

"Fire her up," he calls.

When I turn the key in the ignition this time, I remember to press down on the clutch as well. But Finn's *tough old girl* seems a bit under the weather—literally. She wheezes, then sputters out a wet cough. There is no roar of an engine. No spark. No nothing. I glance back through the rear window at Finn. He gestures for me to try again. I twist the key and hold this time. An unhappy metal-scraping-metal sound complains from under the dented hood. I turn the key back to its starting position, afraid I'm going to blow up the beloved Blazer.

"Third times a charm," Finn calls, and then slaps the rear window.

Squeezing my eyes shut, I turn the key and pray hard. The metal-scraping-metal drowns out the light sounds of the mist and breeze.

"Give her gas," Finn shouts. "Come on. Come on," he chants.

The beast of a vehicle rumbles to life as if she understands Finn.

He flashes a thumbs-up. "You know how to drive a stick, right?"

I shake my head. "Not really," I say, trying not to think about my jerking and stopping and starting back at Zeke's. We should have discussed this before I fired up the beast.

"It's easy. Just let off the clutch and press the gas—gently and at the same time." His head drops from sight in the rearview mirror as he prepares to push.

I let off the clutch a bit, but nothing happens. Biting the inside of my cheek, I apply pressure to the gas—gently like he said. But I'm so focused on my gentle pressing, I lose track of the clutch and release it completely. The car lurches forward.

My chest smashes against the steering wheel. Cursing from behind the Blazer interrupts my wincing.

Glancing in the rearview mirror, I check for Finn. "You okay?" I call.

He coughs and sputters as I put the car in gear and turn off the engine. When I step out, I see him face first in the sand near the rear bumper.

"Finn, I'm so sorry." I rush to help him as he struggles to a seated position.

I offer my hand. He accepts, and I pull him forward.

"Do you want me to try it again?" I ask.

"No." He signals me to halt with one hand and massages his ribs with the other. "Let me try."

I cross my fingers as he slides in behind the steering wheel. He turns the key and *his girl* fires right up. My breath catches, and my chest expands. Sucking down air, I realize it's become almost second nature to hold my breath. Please, please, let him get the Blazer on the road.

The engine revs higher and higher as Finn presses the gas pedal, but the Blazer doesn't budge. He gives her more gas. An angry stream of sand shoots from beneath the back tires. They dig in deeper and deeper. Clamping my mouth shut, I'm right back to holding my breath. I want to scream. Why can't we catch a break?

"Maybe we should just keep moving." I hug myself and rub my upper arms. I'm not exactly drenched, but the mist has picked up. The clouds hang so low I can almost touch them. My clothes and hair act like sponges, absorbing thick moisture from the air.

"No. I have an idea." Determination etches his face. "I've got this."

I follow as he moves toward the back of the vehicle. Opening the rear door a second time, he removes boogie boards, a lacrosse stick, and other sporting equipment I can't identify. He piles everything on the ground beside the car.

I help without speaking, not wanting to interrupt his thinking. Eventually, he uncovers a long wooden board and gives it a tug. But it's stuck, wedged in place beneath a stack of books. Pulling them toward me, I can't help but notice the first title—*To Test or Not to Test: The Pros and Cons of Genetic Counseling.*

I glance over at Finn. In some ways, this ordeal has brought us much closer. I feel like I know him. There's more to him than the class clown he portrays at school. But in other ways, he's as much an enigma as always. I mean, who eats the way he does, lives the way he does, and studies homeopathic medicine *and* genetic counseling?

The top book slips to the sand, unveiling the next title— *Illness in the Family.* Finn looks up. Our eyes lock. His lips part like he wants to say something. His face tightens, as though he's in pain.

"I'm sorry, Finn," I whisper, suddenly understanding what he was trying to tell me back at the cottage about his father's death. There was a lot of pain. I see that clearly now, but he chooses to remember and relive the beauty. In his mind, the beauty and the pain are all woven together like some intricate tapestry. I was listening to only half of what he was saying.

"Sorry about what?" Tilting his head, he releases the board and focuses on me.

I form my words carefully. I can't put a finger on it, but I feel like we're talking two different languages, like if I'm not careful I'm going to say something terribly wrong. "I'm sorry about . . . your dad."

"Yeah. Me too." His shoulders relax as he leans on the bumper.

I point at the stack of books cradled in my arms. "Your dad's illness—it must have been tough. My comments were rude about the way you handled his death. I'm a stubborn, opinionated jerk." My emotions tangle in my stomach. I feel my mouth smiling at the same time my eyes fight back tears. "And I hope you can forgive me, because I've been thinking, and I really want us to be—" I choke on the sob welling in my throat before I can say *together*.

He gently removes the books from my arms and sets them back in the car. Without breaking eye contact, he pulls me to the bumper beside him.

I can't explain what's happening, but something big is coming. I just know it. I've experienced enough tragedy to recognize the sizzle of electricity in the air that precedes bad news. He lifts one of my hands, squeezing it between both of his, and waits for me to meet his eyes. My mind jumps from image to image—waking up facing him on the couch at the first cottage, my feet in his lap at the second house. It keeps returning to our kiss on the beach and in the closet. My lips tingle. Have I done something wrong? Is he mad I said I wasn't sure what I wanted last night?

I've watched enough romantic comedies to know that look on a boy's face. He's about to let me down easy, which is pretty ironic considering I'm the one who's been running away from him. "Sophie, you're smart, pretty . . ."

Okay, now I'm definitely not breathing. I'm certain my

digestive, circulatory, and nervous systems have shut down as well. I'm literally frozen in place.

"I've always liked you—even when you insult my intelligence and think I'm just a big, dumb surfer guy." He bumps his shoulder against mine. "You're the only person who ever really challenged me."

But?

"There's something I need to tell you."

"Okay." I try to sound nonchalant, but my voice cracks. What was I thinking, opening my heart to Finn Sanders? I never should have allowed him to distract me from my primary goal—getting to Manteo and taking care of Mom and Mere. When I blew a tire, I should have set out on foot.

"What you said last night about your dad—and what you told me before about your sister . . . about how you couldn't handle losing anyone else you cared about . . ."

"Finn, spit it out. What are you trying to say?" My pulse churns in my ears, louder than the distant ocean.

"I need to tell you something." Mist glistens like spiders' webs on his eyelashes.

"You said that already."

"Yeah. Right." He's utterly tongue-tied. The boy who never shuts up is speechless. His Adam's apple catches halfway down his neck when he tries to swallow. "It's just that I wasn't completely honest with you about my dad."

"He didn't die of colon cancer?"

"He did, but it wasn't your typical colon cancer. The Lynch syndrome thing I mentioned? It's complicated. I don't think I explained it very well. Or at all."

"Okay." I exhale a little. I remember him saying something

about that when he first told me about his father. Maybe this really isn't about me—about us. It's all about his dad's death. And he just needs to get something off his chest.

"It's a genetic thing. There's a fifty-fifty chance I inherited the gene." He holds my stare, neither of us blinking.

I stay perfectly still, trying to understand what he's saying.

"My dad had an unusually early onset, which means if I inherited the gene, my onset will probably be early—possibly even earlier than his." His stops talking, like he's waiting for me to connect the dots. "It's a really ugly disease, Sophie. After what you said in the closet . . ."

My cheeks warm when he mentions the closet.

"I just thought maybe we shouldn't . . . What I mean is . . . I know you're not the kind of girl to kiss just anyone. And I don't think you'd want to get close to someone who might be checking in at the Horizontal Hilton when you don't have a reservation." One side of his mouth turns up. Obviously, he thinks his joke is clever. When he finally blinks, a tiny drop of mist falls from his lashes to his cheek.

Before I can stop myself, my heart and mind race from visions of his slow death, to me at his funeral, to me curled in a fetal position in my room unable to drag myself out of bed and clean stalls.

"Sophie, say something."

"What is there to say? I don't even know what to think."

"Say you agree or disagree. Say it's a deal breaker, or you don't care—just say something." He shrugs.

Shaking my head, I lick the salty mist from my lips and concentrate on not letting my teeth chatter. Thoughts ricochet in my head, banging against my skull. I like him. I really do. And as much as I hate to admit it, he's right. Everyone dies. I should be big enough and brave enough to face the facts. I can't grieve for Dad and Mere forever. I have to move forward eventually.

But there's a big difference between eventually and right now. And I *can* grieve until Mom and Mere are taken care of. I can stick to my original goals. I can stick to my well-laid plans. I can put off vet school until Mom is more financially stable, until she can afford to pay someone to help with the barn and Mere. And I can certainly put off girlish crushes, no matter how tempting and fun they might be. I can go back to the self-control I was so good at before this stupid storm. I can totally put a stop to the silly idea of learning to open up and take risks. That may work for some people, but I'm not *some people*. I'm the girl with an overworked mom, a disabled sister, and an absentee dad.

Finn wiggles his eyebrows. "Or say I'm irresistible and sexy and you have to be with me no matter what. Just say something."

I don't have the energy to speak, much less laugh. He looks so hopeful. I wish I could at least fake a smile, but I'm completely drained. I thought maybe I was strong enough to do this. I was wrong. I can't. And I need to bring this emotional train to a grinding halt before it runs away and jumps the rails.

"I'm sorry."

With my free hand, I pull at a loose thread on my shirt. It snaps. He shrugs, like my non-answer is no big deal, but the look on his face totally disagrees with his set jaw and dropped shoulders.

His hand grazes mine as he pushes off the bumper. He pulls it away quickly, turning back to the wooden board. We're separated by only a few inches of salty air, but it may as well be the entire Atlantic Ocean.

CHAPTER TWENTY-TWO

Shape your heart to front the hour,
but dream not that the hours will last.

ALFRED, LORD TENNYSON

After a minute of pushing, pulling, and grunting, Finn successfully frees the wooden board from the back of the Blazer. Unable to concentrate on what he's doing with the genetic counseling books staring up at me, I scoot them back where I found them. Now I'm trying to listen to Finn's explanation about the board.

"It's sort of like a reverse lever," he says. Without glancing back at me, he shovels handfuls of sand from under the rear tire.

"Right." I agree, but my heart isn't into his science lesson. Our previous conversation occupies every crevice of my heart and my mind.

"We should get enough traction from this wheel to be out of here in no time."

No. Time.

Chronos.

Kairos.

The mist stops, and the angry sky lightens to a meditative

gray as I contemplate the symbols of growing light and passing time. I feel the day getting away from us as I fidget at the side of the road.

"We're ready," Finn says, gesturing for me to slide into the front seat.

I follow orders, thankful he accepted my lame apology without pressing me for an explanation of exactly what I was sorry about. The Blazer starts on the first try, like it really wants to please him. He deals with the clutch and gas in one smooth motion, the way I mount a horse. The engine revs.

Then bing, bang, boom. She exhales, and we're off. The temporary world and lives we experienced during our crisis slip farther away with each rotation of the tires, like minutes ticked off on a clock.

Finn twists the knob on the radio. Static greets us on every station, and he clicks it off. The tires bump and crack over twigs, patches of sand, and broken glass littering the road. My brain drafts a mental to-do list that could rival Santa's naughty-or-nice scroll. I need to check things at the house, at the barn, at school.

The distance between Finn and me grows as we head south. I stare out the passenger-side window—my body numb, my emotions numb. Everything numb. I squint for signs of our four-legged friend or other survivors. When Finn slams on the brakes, I snap to attention, turning to the road ahead. My seat belt tightens and holds against my chest as I digest the obstacle in our way.

A downed tree blocks the road. Finn puts the car in park, then bangs his fist on the steering wheel. So much for his staying calm during a crisis. His nerves are finally fraying too.

"Now what are we going to do?" I wave my hand toward the tangled mass of limbs and leaves and trunk blocking our path. "There's no way we're moving that."

His fist tightens on the steering wheel as he turns to face me. "Typical."

"What are you talking about?" Now my fists clench beside my thighs.

"Why do you want to give up every time things get hard?"

I realize this isn't just about the tree in the road. I open my mouth, but my tongue seizes. How dare he? Heat rises from my neck to my ears.

I. Am. Not. A. Quitter.

And I resent him saying it. I've never quit on my family. I've never quit on school. I cross my arms with a huff. "I do *not* quit."

"Humph." He places his hand on the door handle, dismissing me.

"You wait just a minute, Finn Sanders." I reach for his arm, but he pulls away, leaving my hand hanging awkwardly in midair. "I am not a quitter," I say.

He turns back to me, eyes narrow. "You're not?"

"No—I'm not. What have I ever quit on?"

The breeze picks up, blowing in through the smashed windshield and ruffling my tangled hair. "You're quitting on us—on friendship or anything else because you're afraid of getting hurt."

"I never said I—"

"You don't have to say anything." He opens his door and steps down to the road. "You quit on your dad."

I shake my head, certain I misunderstood him. I quit on

my dad? I quit on my dad? Of all the nerve. "You don't know what you're talking about, Finn."

"You wrote him off when he hurt you. Will you give *him* another chance?"

"He wrote me off. He doesn't deserve another chance." I can't believe I'm arguing with him. He doesn't know what he's talking about. It's like trying to reason with a child or a crazy person. "And he doesn't want another chance."

"If he did, would you give him one?" There's a challenge in his tone.

I glare at him. I can't answer his stupid question. And I don't appreciate the way he acts like he knows me better than I know myself. And we don't have time for this crap right now.

He doesn't know me that well. Period. End of story.

He steps out of the car and leaves me seething inside. My feet squish in junk food wrappers and rainwater when I shift in my seat. He examines the tree from every angle, then approaches the heavier trunk end and pushes till his face turns red. The tree doesn't budge. He tries the other end. Nothing. He finally resorts to kicking it, which accomplishes nothing. But I bet his toes will be sore for a few days. Worse if they're broken.

He sulks back to the Blazer, seemingly none the worse. "It's not moving."

Seventeen sarcastic comments pepper my tongue, but I bite them back.

"We've got two options—leave the car and find transportation on the other side . . ." He slides into the driver's seat.

"Or?"

"Or find a chainsaw."

When he slicks his wet hair back and away from his eyes, I see the full weight of his stress. He looks way more man than boy. This storm has aged him as well.

I speak slowly and carefully. "Or we could walk the entire way—not steal anything or vandalize anything else."

He rakes his already raked hair, pausing to grip his head for a minute before continuing. "Or . . ."

He releases his head and pumps the gas. The engine revs. My heart tightens. He grins, like the psycho dad in that Stephen King movie. He extends his arm in front of my chest. A second later, we're crashing into the tree, our necks snapping from the impact. Fortunately, we didn't have enough space to build up much speed, so he didn't kill us. Unfortunately, we didn't have enough space to build up much speed, and the tree didn't budge.

"Have you completely lost your freaking mind?" He is out of control.

Ignoring my question, he turns the key in the ignition. The Blazer sputters and dies.

"We know your mom and sister evacuated safely. We should have gone to get Zeke *first*. He has a chainsaw and supplies and better transportation. Though this storm was also worse than we thought it would be . . ."

I tried to tell him the storm was going to be bad, but I keep my mouth shut.

"I have to make sure he's okay," he says.

"I know you do." I'm tired of arguing. That doesn't make me a quitter. It makes me . . . tired. I blink back tears, determined not to cry now. "I just . . . I need to find my mom."

"And I need to find Zeke. But I guess I'll do that after I

deal with this tree and get you to Manteo." He steps out of the vehicle, striding toward the tree still without so much as a limp. So much for the broken toe hypothesis. He vaults the tree like it's nothing and heads up the center line of the road on the other side.

As he walks away, I realize I need to let him find his uncle. All we've managed to do today is argue, and I can't take it anymore. I need to find Mom and Mere on my own.

I survey the mess that is his car, the mess that is my current reality. I contemplate just getting out. Heading my own way. The storm has passed. Finn and I don't truly owe each other anything now. He can take care of himself and go find Zeke. I can take care of myself and my people. We can pretend none of this ever happened. I mean what happened, really?

Two frightened people trapped alone in a storm kissed. Not much of a big deal in that. So maybe we exposed a few emotions as well. That's not anything that wouldn't happen in a game of truth or dare or around a bonfire or whatever.

He's fire. I'm ice. We're night and day, water and oil, and every other cliché ever written about opposites. Leaving now is logical—like ripping off a Band-Aid. Leaving now is practical and cautious. And I don't care what Finn says. Being cautious is not the same as quitting.

Being cautious is wise.

But . . .

No buts, Sophie.

I wait for him to turn down a side road before reaching for the door handle. Then, holding my breath, I pull the handle and the heavy door creaks a warning. I freeze, but Finn doesn't come running back to me.

I step down to the asphalt. As I carefully close the door, a worm of guilt wiggles in my gut. I can't just walk out on him. We've been in this together. Plus, I don't want him to be right. I don't want to be a quitter. Ugh.

I find a dry scrap of paper and a colored pencil in his console and leave a quick note telling him to go find Zeke and assuring him I'll be fine.

Pushing the door open, I step down to the road again. This time I slam the door without peering back inside. As I tromp away from the Blazer, I ignore the rear windows and the books piled there.

Determination sets in. My head and feet make a decision before my heart has time to sway them.

With Mere's compass tucked in my pocket, I widen the chasm between Finn and me. Even the wind seems to be against me as I head south. It impedes my progress, literally pushing against my forward momentum and scraping my ankles with bits of sand. I clench and unclench my fists. I'm cold. I'm tired. Honestly, I'm not even sure I can make it the rest of the way.

I tell myself my normal world and predictable routine are just across the bridge at the southern tip of this island. All I have to do now is figure out how to get there on my own.

CHAPTER TWENTY-THREE

My life has crept so long
on a broken wing . . .

ALFRED, LORD TENNYSON

I trudge south, contemplating the last few days, contemplating the grumbling of the ocean and the swooshing of the sea-grass and the weight of the heavy air. It's hard to believe the amount of sand that's been displaced and redeposited by the storm. Just moving sand—not to mention clearing downed trees and power lines, repairing roofs, and rebuilding homes—will take residents ages to complete.

As I walk, I listen carefully, telling myself I'm listening for the sound of rescue personnel or the horse. If I'm honest, though, I have to admit I'm listening for the Blazer and Finn chasing after me, begging me for another chance. In reality that would only make things more difficult, and yet I can't help my traitorous heart.

But I don't have to worry about what to say to him because the wind and waves make the only sounds in my world.

Rubbing my thumb back and forth against the compass in my pocket, I count the broken yellow stripes in the middle of the road. My stomach grumbles. Too bad I didn't snag a granola bar before heading out on my great, solitary adventure. I lose count of the yellow lines somewhere around two hundred and twenty and start again at one.

A foreign thump breaks the monotony of the ocean's somber melody, and I jump a foot in the air. If it's Finn, I don't know what I'll say—how I'll explain setting out on my own. I hear it again, and it's not his beloved Blazer. It's something even better. It's the unmistakable thump of a helicopter. My heart rises above the fog and mist as I bolt toward higher ground on my left. Clawing and scrabbling for the top of the dunes, I cup my hands over my eyebrows, straining for better visibility.

Brushing sand from my hands and arms, I squint out to sea and spy what looks like an intoxicated housefly zigging and zagging over the open ocean. It must be the Coast Guard, but they're totally not searching for stranded islanders. Someone or something must be lost at sea. I shiver, trying to imagine surviving the brutal tumult of the Atlantic in anything smaller than the aircraft carrier Dad and I toured in Virginia Beach two summers ago.

I watch until the helicopter disappears completely from view and swipe hot tears from my face. Up here, perched on a high dune, I have a clear view of the ravenous storm surge. I have no idea what time it is. I don't even remember where I last saw my phone. Was it that first night at the cottage?

A shadow of movement catches my eyes near the frothy bubbles at the high tide mark. Shaking my head, I blink to clear my vision, sure my eyes are playing tricks on me. It's the chestnut horse Finn and I saved from the silt fence. He's favoring his back leg and not moving very fast. But he survived. He really, truly survived.

The horse spots me dancing and swinging my arms over my head and stops to stare, ears flicking back and forth as he assesses the situation. My celebration is short-lived when I realize the poor guy can't have found fresh water. Years ago, the horses pawed through the sand for freshwater drinking holes. But I don't think horses can balance on only two legs. Plus, these animals have become a bit acclimated to human support. I can't remember if the Wild Horse Fund volunteers provide freshwater sources, but I can't risk it. It could be days before rescue workers find him—if they find him. Their first priority will be human survivors.

The weight of the situation presses down on my shoulders and on the rest of me as I track the horse's slow progress in the sand. He turns his heavy head and takes a faltering step, obviously deciding the crazy girl on the dunes is too far away to present much of a threat. I glance south toward Manteo. The magnetic force of Mom and Mere tugs on my heart.

Lifting my shoulders, I turn toward the most important people in my life. When I do, I almost step on a perfectly formed sand dollar. It's still gray. We haven't had enough sun or heat in recent days to bleach and harden the brittle shell. But it's miraculous that such a delicate creature could survive the crashing surf and still wash up intact.

Then a kaleidoscope of memories punches me in the gut, taking me back to the day Dad left. There was a sand dollar that day too. I'd found several conch shells and a sand dollar while walking alone on the beach. I was bringing them home to Mere and found Dad leaving. We argued. Pointing at the sand dollar in my hand, he said things weren't always as they appeared.

"Some people are just really good at seeing what they want to see," I'd shouted.

He plucked the delicate treasure from my grasp, cracked it into two halves, and tapped one half on his palm. Then he reminded me about the five doves at the center of the starfish and explained how everyone tries so hard to find and preserve the shell that they forget about the beauty at its heart.

I told him if there was beauty in his heart, he wouldn't abandon his wife and children.

He said, "Your mother's tough, Soph. She can take care of herself and what's left of our family."

"Is that your excuse for leaving us?" I screamed at the top of my lungs, effectively silencing him.

When he leaned forward to hug me, I whispered, "I hate you."

And we haven't spoken since.

As much as I hate to admit he's right, he is. Mom is way tougher than the sand dollar at my feet. It dawns on me that my mother may not need me as much as I need her to need me. All this time alone with nothing but my thoughts is making me crazy. Either that, or Finn and all his meditative psychobabble are messing with my head. It doesn't really matter whether Dad's right or Finn's right. The truth is I can't do anything to help Mom or Mere right now. I couldn't do anything to save Mere in the accident. I couldn't stop Dad from walking out on us.

But I can help that horse.

I remember something else—something my favorite teacher

said in middle school. We were collecting money for a homeless shelter up north. She and the other kids were so excited we had collected almost a thousand dollars. She asked me why I wasn't joining the celebration. I told her it wouldn't be enough to take care of the huge homeless problem in the city. I expected her to disagree—to feed me a motivational quote or something. But she told me she understood exactly what I was saying, then proceeded to share her philosophy—that God doesn't expect us to take care of *all* the problems in the world. He expects us to help the specific people placed in our lives and on our hearts. The Richmond homeless shelter was placed on our hearts when one of the girls in our class lost her father there. He overdosed and died sad and alone in that shelter.

I totally get what she was saying now. I can't help *all* the wild horses. I can't do a lot of things right now. But I can help *that* horse—the one that's been placed in my life a second time in as many days. I can steer him toward the safety of his herd north of the fence. I can find freshwater for him. And that's exactly what I'm going to do. I'm not quite sure how, but I'll figure something out. At home with buckets and oats, this would be much simpler. But if I want to be a vet someday, I have to learn how to help all the animals in need, not just the easy ones.

And I am not—repeat, *am not*—a quitter.

CHAPTER TWENTY-FOUR

If you don't concentrate on what you are doing then the thing that you are doing is not what you are thinking.

ALFRED, LORD TENNYSON

I follow the hobbling horse as the mist picks up and the wind shifts. My feet drag the sand. Because of high tide and the angry storm surge, I have to hug the dunes, which means loose sand, which means more effort. We finally near what appears to be a weathered house in the distance. My shoulder shrieks in protest, but I refuse to listen.

The horse hasn't wavered from his northward march, following the pencil-line path between surf and dunes. I know what I must do—employ the ole toilet tank water recovery mission a second time. I hunch forward and drag myself step-by-step up and over the dunes, onto the boardwalk, and to the leaning tower of cedar-sided gray wood posing as a summer home.

The storm already shattered several windows, so reaching through the door and letting myself in hardly even feels like breaking and entering. Either that or my moral compass has completely failed. I slosh through standing water in the living room, soggy books and magazines swishing in my wake. I spot a half bath off the side of the living room and splash in that direction. An overturned plastic trash can rests beside the toilet. I grab it, make sure it's empty, then fill it with water from the toilet tank. Carrying the water down the uneven boardwalk to the beach without spilling it requires balance and upper-body strength, both of which I'm short on today. But somehow I suck it up and press forward, trying not to think about my shoulder injury or slipping and breaking my neck. If the horse weren't injured worse than me, I would never catch him.

But I do. My superhuman determination to save him and prove to myself and maybe Finn that I'm not a quitter fuels my charge up the beach. It does nothing to ease my huffing and puffing or grunting and groaning. As I close in, the horse seems to dig into a reserve of his own and picks up his pace. I'm close enough now to make out the oozing flesh on his back leg. But once I'm within about thirty feet, I can't seem to shrink the gap any farther.

This isn't going to work.

The average horse is used to following, not leading. That's why a wild horse can't survive without a herd. Their herding instinct, which shares a lot of similarities with a game of follow-the-leader, is as strong as their fight-or-flight instinct. As long as I approach from behind, he's going to keep moving away from me faster and faster until he can't take another step. I need to be ahead of him so I can place the water in his direct path, then pray his survival instinct is enough to make him drink.

I decide to try something that works with my own horses.

Normally a human must have a bond with a horse to activate his desire to follow, but I don't have any other genius ideas here. The humming wind and the mist hanging in the air are going to make it difficult for the horse to hear my movements. But it can't hurt to try.

I stop and pause to the count of ten. As I turn around, I pray for the best. After several steps in the opposite direction, I peek over my shoulder. And miracle of miracles, my horse-whisperer plan kind of worked. The horse didn't turn to follow me. I didn't expect him to. But he did at least stop. He has to need a break himself. Even from thirty-plus feet, I can see his ribs rising and falling with each labored breath. His head hangs low. He makes no effort to avoid the frothy waves lapping at his hooves.

Hot beads of sweat form at my hairline, mixing with the chilly drizzle. Carrying several gallons of water is taking its toll. Acting quickly to take advantage of his stillness, I scurry back up and over the dunes. He's blocked from my sight as I head north, parallel to the dunes.

"Don't move, big guy. Don't move," I plead as I hurry forward.

The short trek constricts my lungs and cramps my muscles. I force myself to go an extra five to ten yards to be safe before hefting my heavy feet and legs back up and over the dunes.

"Thank you. Thank you," I whisper to the wind when I realize I have in fact gotten in front of the pony. He lifts his head a bit as I approach, his ears flicking in my direction.

"Easy, big guy. Easy." I keep my voice low and my speech slow as I take another half step in his direction. "Easy."

His head turns to the right on his long neck as though he's

contemplating a retreat, but his legs remain locked firmly in place. The wild look is gone from his eyes. No white is visible now. Actually, his eyes are oddly sunken back in his head, a sure sign of severe dehydration. I notice he's either drifted closer to shore or the tide's coming in again, because the water is splashing higher and higher on his legs. I need to hurry.

I inch forward as far as I dare and deposit the trash can as close to him as possible. Before withdrawing, I splash my hand around in the water, hoping to interest him. His ears flick, and he lowers his head an inch or two. I climb halfway up the dune at my back and plop butt-first in the sand—partially to give him space, partially because if I don't sit down I'm going to die.

The horse doesn't move, and I feel sick to my stomach. All this time, all this effort, and it hasn't done any good. Dropping my face in my hands, I let the hot tears overflow my eyes and seep between my fingers. I really just want to lie down and sleep. When the breeze shifts, I lift my head and see the horse has moved within inches of the trash can.

I hold my breath. Digging my hands in the sand near my legs, I will him to close the gap. He half hops, half steps to the trash can, and a fresh wave of tears spills down my cheeks.

The splitting pain in my shoulder and calves from climbing up and down the dunes is worth it. When he drops his head and slurps water from the plastic trash can, my heart glides out to sea like the albatross Finn and I spotted yesterday. If I can get a wild horse to drink from a trash can in close proximity to me, surely I can get him to safety north of the sound-to-sea fence. Then it's due south for me. Do not pass go. Do not collect two hundred dollars. Get to Mom and Mere and our own horses and put our lives back into order.

The horse drains the trash can, then flicks it to the side with his nose. Neither of us moves for several long minutes. After giving us both a chance to rest, I move in a few steps from behind the exhausted horse. I hate to push him in his condition, but I need to get him to safety. Thankfully, he plows ahead when I approach from behind. The water seems to have refreshed him a bit, and the salty wash of surf on his lower legs seems to have cleaned his wounds and possibly even lessened the pain.

He's not setting any records, but he hobbles forward at a steady rate. I struggle to keep up. When I swipe the water from my cheeks and forehead, my forehead feels hot—steamy. I shake it off, quickly dismissing the alarm bells that start ringing in my head. My senses are probably still a bit off from the loss of blood and shock. Besides, I seriously doubt an infection could set in this quickly. I probably need rest and lots of water myself. If I do get an infection, which is pretty common in post-hurricane nastiness, that's what antibiotics are for. I'll be fine for a few more hours, and this guy needs me.

I dig deep into my last reserves and press forward. Each step is like trying to swim through chocolate pudding. We struggle along in silence, our roles reversed in this backward game of follow-the-leader. With single-minded focus, I advance from one hoof print to the next, counting as I go. At three hundred and eight, my right calf cramps. There's no way I'm going to make it all the way to the fence. Lifting my eyes from the charcoal sand littered with shell fragments, twisted cans, broken bottles, and God knows what else, I look for somewhere to sit. A nice hunk of driftwood would be dreamy. Something brown up ahead catches my eye. I shake my head.

It can't be what I think it is.

But it is.

It's the freaking fence. The fence. The fence. I find my seventieth wind and press forward despite the knotted muscle in my leg.

We did it. We did it.

I did it.

If I had the energy, I'd dance, or flip, or even just fist bump the turbulent air. Instead I rest my hands on my thighs and breathe a sigh of relief. My joy deflates as I scan the fence.

Yes, we made it.

But there's no break in sight, no wild horses in sight, which means I have no safe place to deposit my new friend.

We've traveled all this way for nothing.

CHAPTER TWENTY-FIVE

*The shell must break
before the bird can fly.*

ALFRED, LORD TENNYSON

When cold water brushes my feet, my eyes fly open, and I lift the side of my face from the sand where I collapsed. My shoulder throbs. The ocean roars. I just want to go home. But that's not an option, and neither is lying here and drowning. So I brace my hands in the sand and push up to my knees. Sand cakes every crack and crevice of my body. I need a hot shower or ten.

Rising unsteadily from the sand, I spy my wild pal. His head swivels in my direction. If I didn't know better, I'd swear he was shaking his head at me.

"I know. I know. I'm pathetic," I say to him, a little concerned about my mental stability. I can't remember the last time I ate or drank anything. It seems like it was ages ago. My world has been reduced to jagged, chopped-off ridges of sand, roiling waves, and flattened and sideways houses. And this horse.

"Let's do this." I wave my arms in his direction. He plods forward as though he knows the drill, and he looks much better than I feel. With the fence guiding him on one side and me on the other, slightly behind, it's much easier to steer him in the direction I want him to go. He got out somehow, and I'm going to find the break he escaped through if it kills me.

It might.

The farther we travel, the more I begin to wonder if this is a lost cause. If he swam around the fence, which is highly unlikely, or jumped it, which is technically impossible, I've got a big problem. My epic rescue will be an epic fail without some way of crossing the fence.

Lost in thought and trying to calculate how much fence I have left to inspect, I don't realize my buddy has stopped till I'm almost within arm's reach of his hindquarters. He lifts his head, trying to get a read on something in the distance. His ears twitch back and forth between me and a new development up ahead.

I squint but don't see anything but an endless landscape of sand and clouds and a straight, unbroken line of fence. Horses have better hearing and smell than humans, so maybe he's zeroing in on something he can't even see. My heart lifts at the possibility that maybe the Coast Guard helicopter has turned inland.

Determined we must be nearing the end of this trek, I swish my hands toward his rump, encouraging him to proceed. My hamstrings protest as we ascend what must be the spine of the island. Then we're descending on the other side, and the protest transfers to the fronts of my thighs as I brace myself against gravity. Honestly, it would be easier to roll or stumble down the dune, but I don't want to frighten my charge. As I contemplate sitting for a second, a new sound interrupts the rush of wind and waves, rumbling in the background despite our distance from the sea.

It's a mechanical whining—not a helicopter, not a boat, more like a car. But there's no way anyone's up here in a car. It would take some powerful all-wheel drive to reach this part of the island. I'm not even sure Dad's truck or Finn's Blazer would make it up here.

But someone or something has to be operating that engine—hopefully a fireman or an EMT. At the bottom of the ridge, the noise grows louder. As we round a clump of scrub brush, an absurd monster truck materializes in the distance. The tires stand taller than I do, above my head. Some sort of thick canvas webbing fills the side windows in place of glass. Based on the various colors of the rusty cab and bed, I'm pretty sure the thing was pieced together from the corpses of trucks that haven't seen anything but the back lot of a junkyard for the last few years, possibly the last few decades.

If there's a live person to go with the Franken-truck, I have no choice. I must proceed. I could use some help here, and that scary excuse for a vehicle might be my ticket to the mainland.

"Hello," I call, but the trifecta of wind, sea, and monster truck completely drown out my voice.

I inhale deeply, cup my hands around my mouth, and call again. "Hello!"

Nothing.

As I suck in a lungful of air and prepare to scream at the top of my lungs, the engine stops, and a *Duck Dynasty* beard with a wiry body attached to it steps out of the truck. Holy crap! If I weren't so mentally and physically exhausted, I might laugh or cry. Instead, I simply stare. The irony of the universe is not wasted on me when I realize the man scurrying toward us is Finn's uncle, Zeke—the same Zeke I said could fend for himself, the same Zeke I chose to head away from in favor of the mainland and my mother and sister. I roll my eyes at the heavens.

"Over here!" He waves his hands over his head as if I could miss his beard. Or his truck. His enthusiasm throws me off balance. I'm not sure whether it's some strange side effect of the storm, or surprise, or what, but this Zeke is way happier to see me than the Zeke of two days ago. He jogs across the sand to meet us, and the wild horse whinnies softly, almost as if he recognizes Zeke, which is impossible. There is no way these two know each other.

"Guillermo! Guillermo!" Zeke's happier than I've seen him, like he's reconnecting with a lost loved one instead of a strange girl and a bedraggled horse. "Guillermo, you made it, buddy. I was looking for you."

He has eyes only for the horse. My fatigued brain struggles to keep up as he approaches and pats my *wild* horse on the shoulder. I begin to doubt everything I've always believed about these horses. And now I'm really skeptical of Zeke as well. I'm pretty sure he can get in big trouble with Fish and Game and the cops for interfering with these protected animals.

When he finally makes eye contact, I realize he has a mouth, and lips, and teeth, because there's something resembling a smile behind all that hair. But it fades quickly.

"I thought you guys evacuated." His eyes dart to the stand of scrubby trees behind me. "Where's Finn?"

That's a really good question with no really good answer. "We wrecked. We stayed in a house south of here during the storm . . ."

His eyes narrow on my face as he runs a leathery hand through his beard. "So where's Finn?"

"We . . . uh . . . separated . . ."

"Why in the—" He stops himself before the profanity flies and glances at the horse like he's afraid he'll spook him. "Why would you do that?"

Because I wanted to. Because I can take care of myself.

Because maybe I'm afraid of getting close to Finn, which makes him kind of right and me all wrong, and kind of a liar, and maybe even a quitter.

I shrug. That's all I can do with my heart deflating inside my chest.

"So where is he?" Clearly, he's not going to let it go, and I can't blame him.

"Looking for a chainsaw to clear a road." I shake my head, unable to hide my irritation.

"And you?" He gestures from me to the horse.

"And I what?"

"And you just happened to pair up with Guillermo here and head away from civilization." His eyebrows drop so low, they may meet the beard, swallow his face, and blind him for all eternity.

"It's kind of a long story." I shift my weight from one tired leg to the other.

"We've got nothing but time." He studies Guillermo's back leg, frowning, and waits for me to answer.

Actually, *he* may have nothing but time. I really need to get to the mainland.

He crosses his arms in front of his chest, like he can wait all day, and I cave.

"I was headed to the mainland, but I saw him." I gesture to my wild horse friend, who Zeke keeps calling Guillermo. "Finn and I saw the horse before—caught in a silt fence."

Massaging his chest with his fist, Zeke waits for me to continue. Concern etches his face.

"He was tangled badly and making his leg worse struggling to free himself. Then I was heading south today and saw him again. He was dehydrated, and I knew he wouldn't survive without his herd."

"That's pretty impressive you decided to help him." His forehead rises, revealing his eyes again. My chest expands a little.

"Well, my parents invested a lot of their lives into protecting those horses and building that fence." I nod toward the power cable barrier to my right.

"What's your name again?" he asks, rubbing Guillermo between the ears.

"Sophie. Sophie March."

His eyes widen. "You Doug March's girl?"

"Yes." I wait for him to explain how he knows my dad.

"Your dad and I went to school together. We made rescue calls together before the fence went up. He's cool—haven't seen him in a while, though."

Me neither.

"I heard he hit on hard times." He shakes his head. "Your daddy was the only person other than family to visit me in rehab. He was always the first person to lend a hand when one of our buddies needed help. He's done a lot of good, that man. Hope you and your pretty mama are giving him lots of support when he needs it."

I don't answer. I can't. A butterfly of guilt flaps its wings in my chest, initiating a tiny waft of air. Zeke is right. My dad was always there for everyone until the wreck. He was always there for me, Mom, and Mere. He never missed a single Daddy and Donuts in elementary school. Never missed a father-daughter dance. Never ignored us to play golf or watch football. Mom said he was her knight in shining armor—until he wasn't.

"And I haven't seen you since you were knee-high to a grasshopper. Never would've recognized you. You were a little show-off, always trying to impress your daddy. Kept him on his toes too—running after you about as much as the horses, if I remember correctly."

With no means of escape from my tight chest, the puff of butterfly wind in my lungs begins to swirl in a circular motion.

"Yeah." I force out the single syllable.

I haven't thought about my childhood relationship with Dad in a long time—how he and I were the two amigos. Back then, Mere was more likely to stay home with Mom, where she could dance when she finished working around the house or barn. They were joined at the hip. I wanted to be in the truck with Dad, windows rolled down, racing head-on to a new adventure.

It's funny what a difference a decade makes—how the years work on us like an ocean current shaping, moving, and reshaping a sandbar. It's mind-boggling to think how quickly your entire life can change. If there hadn't been an accident on the bypass that day, Dad wouldn't have been on the beach road. If he hadn't been distracted by the change of plans, or his phone, or whatever, maybe he and Mere wouldn't have wrecked. Even if they had still wrecked, maybe he wouldn't have let the guilt eat him alive if he hadn't been messing with his phone around the time of the accident. I doubt anyone except Dad will ever know for sure exactly what happened that day. Maybe he was telling the truth when he said it all happened too fast to remember the details. I'm too physically and emotionally exhausted to think about it right now.

Whatever happened, he let it eat at him, and his solution was prescription pain meds and alcohol. I could forgive him for anything—the addiction, the depression, anything—but I could not forgive him for walking out.

"I don't recognize you either," I say, trying to sound casual and ignore the cyclone of emotions churning inside of me.

"Back then, I had more hair up here." He smiles and pats the top of his head. "And less here." He tugs on his beard.

I have no response for that. "So about Guillermo—what do you propose we do?"

"He's a young male, so that makes it tough," Zeke says, then runs his hand along Guillermo's rump. "The stallion in the band runs off the young males when they near maturity. Generally, these guys take up with a band of other bachelors until they can recruit a harem of their own. But this guy's been hanging around the shack. I've tried to ignore him, but he's still too comfortable with humans and will probably have to be rehomed."

"How are we going to get him back to his herd?" I nod toward the fence, ready to get this show on the road and for a minute to gather my thoughts. It's hard to think properly with this strange hermit staring me down—a strange hermit who's not acting hermit-y at all because he likes my dad and because I earned some respect for risking my safety to protect a wild horse.

"One thing at a time. We need to find Finn, and I need to

know where you found Guillermo," he says, not answering my question.

"I'm pretty sure Finn can take care of himself." Unless some gnarly waves distract him, or he amputates his leg with a chainsaw, or he runs off the road in a *borrowed* vehicle. For a second, I really miss him. I mean, we were kind of a good team. He brought out some of the adventurous little girl tucked so deep inside of me, I'd completely forgotten she was there.

"I know we were south of Duck but not sure how far south." I shrug. It doesn't seem that important now that we're back here at the fence. Zeke rests his hand on Guillermo's rump as he leans in for a closer inspection of the wound. "Let me clean that wound and give him some water. Then we find Finn. Then we take it from there."

"I really need to get the horse to safety so I can find my mom." I glance at his monster truck, hoping he'll offer me a ride to Manteo.

"*Safety* is an interesting term under the circumstances."

"Yeah." He's not getting the I-need-a-ride facial clues, so I cut to the point. "Look, my mom and sister need me. Can you get me to Manteo?"

"Sure—after we get Guillermo squared away." He twists the tip of his long beard around his index finger as he stares off into the distance. "And find Finn."

I try to be patient. I do. But I can't stand it any longer. "Do you at least have a phone I can use?"

"No signal up here even without a hurricane." He shrugs.

Without responding, I blink and step toward the truck. I don't have the energy to respond. I barely have the energy to drag myself across the sand to lean on one of the giant tires.

I've given one hundred percent and then some, and it still wasn't enough. My blood, sweat, and tears weren't enough. I'm not enough—never was, never will be.

I'm done.

What's the point in fighting Mother Nature? Zeke? Finn?

There is no point. I'm completely at their mercy.

Closing my eyes, I slide toward the sand until my butt rests on the lower half of the tire.

I'm defeated.

I quit.

CHAPTER TWENTY-SIX

Knowledge comes, but wisdom lingers.

ALFRED, LORD TENNYSON

As I cross my arms and settle in to wait for the next wave of emotional turmoil, the sound of a gunshot breaks the air. My heart skips a beat. "Wh-what was that?" I ask. With my heart lodged firmly in my throat, I jump from Zeke's unsteady chair. It's like I'm stuck in some survival reality TV show. Every time I overcome some great obstacle or press through some physical or emotional challenge, the producers throw in another insane trial.

Zeke hums and pours liniment on Guillermo's leg. He doesn't even look up from his work. He's completely unfazed, as if the sound of a gunshot on an isolated northern beach in the wake of a hurricane is nothing to be concerned about. Even Guillermo seems untroubled by the noise.

Finally, Zeke smiles at me, seeming to have sensed my fear. "It's just Finn's car backfiring. That kid's amazing. He found us."

Is amazing really a suitable adjective for Finn? Maybe frustrating or shocking or . . . sort of amazing.

Sure enough, a few seconds later, the vomit-green Blazer

rumbles into sight, barreling around the scrub brush in the distance. She looks more horrendous than usual with broken glass for a windshield, and she kind of lists to one side like two of her tires are flat.

To my utter surprise, I feel my face break into a goofy smile. And Yesenia's all-time favorite Tennyson quote repeats in my head. I can hear her as though she's standing beside me. "'Tis better to have loved and lost than never to have loved at all."

I always thought that particular tidbit was a pile of romantic mumbo jumbo. Now I'm not so sure. Right this second, with Guillermo, who I feel at least partially responsible for saving, close by and Finn approaching, I totally get it. It's about taking risks as much as it's about love. It's better to take a risk and fail than to live in fear.

I hope Finn and I can make amends and at least be friends. Yesenia and Tennyson are right. I've learned from him, from our time together, from this stupid storm. I never would have wished for this hurricane. I never would have wished for a flat tire or a horse to be caught in a fence and injured. But I can learn from these experiences. I've learned a lot about taking risks for myself and for others. Now it's time to take the risk to end all risks.

After what seems like ages but is probably just a minute or two, the Blazer stops a few yards from us, sputters, and then dies. The door opens with a painful groan as Finn steps down to the sand.

He jogs toward me, his face quickly transforming from surprise to skepticism. "You're here."

"I'm here." I hold his eyes, willing him to keep an open mind. To understand that I'm not going anywhere anymore.

He nods, then steps toward Zeke. "I've been looking for you everywhere." He slaps Zeke on the back. Then his head jerks back in my direction. "Isn't this the horse that was tangled in the fence?"

"Yes."

"And you two tamed him, or what?"

"It's a long story," Zeke and I answer in unison. I shrug. He chuckles a bit.

Finn glances back and forth between me and Zeke, like he's contemplating what happened between the two of us while he was gone.

"So what now?" Finn asks.

As much as I want to race to Manteo, I know I couldn't live with myself if we left Guillermo alone up here. "We find the break in the fence and get the horse back where he belongs."

Zeke caps the bottle of liniment and turns toward me. "There's no break in the fence."

"There has to be. How else would a horse get over here?" I ask, circling back to the real discussion.

"I don't know."

I try not to roll my eyes, but this conversation feels like it's about to derail.

"It doesn't really matter, does it—how he got over here. What's done is done." Zeke puts down the liniment bottle, hitches up his Hawaiian shorts, and turns back to Guillermo, who stands dozing near the fence. "What matters is how we deal with the present situation and how we get him north of that fence."

"How're we going to do that without a break in the fence?" I glance at Finn, willing him to jump in and help.

"We break it ourselves, herd him through. Then you two head to Manteo, and I'll stay here until rescuers arrive."

My brain says his plan is ridiculous. My gut says it might just work.

"That fence is solid. How do you plan to take it down?" I turn to Zeke, praying he has a good answer.

"We could dig up two posts and push them down with both vehicles, but that could take several hours." He rubs his beard.

I don't have several hours. I need to let Mom and Mere know I'm okay. I'm glad I got the horse to Zeke. I'm glad Finn found us. I would make the same choices if I had to do it all over again. But there has to be a faster way.

"What if we skip the digging part and just use the trucks to knock down a couple of posts?" I say. I thought Finn was being an idiot when he crashed into the fallen tree in an attempt to move it, and now that's exactly what I'm suggesting—using not one but two vehicles as battering rams. But I don't see any other way.

No one speaks for several seconds. A steady wind ruffles Guillermo's tail and Zeke's beard, but it's no longer the god-awful gale of the hurricane. I roll my head from side to side, trying to loosen the knots in my lower neck and shoulders.

"It could work," Finn says. "But if we wreck the trucks beyond repair, it could be another day before we get to Manteo."

Ugh. Good point.

He pushes black hair away from his face, revealing the knot on his forehead. The thing is still massive, but it's even more yellow-green now, not purple-black. I find myself feeling relieved.

Finn points at the gray sky like he has a genius idea. "What if we use the Blazer to push and save Zeke's truck for pulling?" He points at the rusty but huge winch on the back of Zeke's Franken-truck.

"Let's do it," Zeke says, then claps his hands. "Finn, you push. I'll pull. Sophie, you keep an eye on Guillermo."

Shaking my head, I meet his eyes. "No. Guillermo is more comfortable with you. You keep an eye on him. I'll help Finn with the fence," I say, placing my hands on my hips Wonder-Woman style, ready to stand my ground if he argues.

Zeke glances at Finn with raised eyebrows.

Finn nods. "If she says she can do it, I trust her."

And just like that, we're ready to save Guillermo for good—that is, of course, if I can drive Franken-truck and kick this fence's butt.

I haven't felt like kicking much butt lately, but suddenly I'm ready to give it a whirl.

A few minutes later, I'm banging my fist on the steering wheel, gritting my teeth, and screaming, "Come on. Come on."

This has to work. It has to.

I believed. I trusted. I took a risk. But the fence post is *not* budging. I peek in the rearview mirror to see if Finn's making more progress than me in his Blazer. Then I take a deep breath and prepare to drive Franken-truck forward one more time. Between the dirt on my rear window, the jagged glass in his windshield, and the shaggy black hair falling in his face, I can't read his facial expression. But I can read my own. It looks like it's about to crumple in on itself—much like the crumpled front end of Finn's Blazer.

"Ugggh! Come on!" The screaming originates from somewhere deeper than my throat. It's more of a fierce growl than individual words. My upper body jerks back and forth, slamming the seat behind me despite my still-tender shoulder.

As I will the behemoth forward, I press the gas pedal halfway to the floor. The engine screams louder than I do, threatening to rip out from under the hood if I give it more gas. If I blow up this truck, we're in deep trouble. We have no back-up plan. The Blazer might have one more semi-solid push on the post in her before she's immobile and wrecked beyond repair.

My pulse throbs in my neck. Zeke stands in the distance, too far away to yell advice over the earsplitting engine, too far away for me to make out his facial expression either. I look to Finn in the rearview mirror a second time. I think he nods.

And I go for it.

I just do it.

I stomp on the gas.

The truck rocks and bucks. The engine shrieks. But nothing happens. The post doesn't budge.

"Grrrrrr." Hanging on to the steering wheel for dear life, I lift my butt off the seat for better leverage and manage to press the gas pedal the last half-centimeter to the floor. In the time it takes me to blink, the truck lurches forward, rocketing across the sand. My heart races. The truck races. But my brain remains frozen, suspended for a millisecond before it fires the signal to my foot to brake.

Lifting my foot off the gas, I stomp the brake, desperate to stop before I hit the stand of saplings and scrub brush head-on. The truck halts suddenly, and the massive fence post whiplashes, smacking the back of the truck with enough force to slam me chest first into the steering wheel.

CHAPTER TWENTY-SEVEN

Words, like nature, half reveal and half conceal the soul within.

ALFRED, LORD TENNYSON

grip my side, gasping for air, but nothing's happening. I can't breathe. I can't speak.

I collapse against the seat. When I do, my lungs open enough to suck in half a breath. Something's squeezing my chest. I struggle to breathe. "Oh, God!" I moan, certain I've injured myself. But each plea for help carries a bit more oxygen to my lungs, and I realize I haven't broken ribs or punctured a lung. I knocked the wind out of myself.

I close my eyes and concentrate on inhaling and exhaling.

"Sophie? Sophie! Are you okay?"

I open one eye. Finn stands on the running board, peering in at me. If his eyes open any wider, they might pop out of his face.

I strain to form something resembling a smile, but don't have the energy. "I knew you cared, Wild Man," I croak.

"Not funny. You scared the crap out of me. I thought you hurt yourself or—" His jaw clenches, like he's imagining the worst.

"I'm surprised you didn't try mouth-to-mouth," I say, my voice a tiny bit less bull-froggy.

He jerks as if I slapped him, then squints at me carefully. "Wait. Was that a joke?"

A genuine smile tugs at the corners of my mouth. "Yeah. Yeah, it was."

When he drops from the running board to the sand, we're eye level. "And you took down that beast of a fence."

He lifts the door handle, pulling the door open.

I shake my head. "*We* took down the fence."

He lifts my arm from the steering wheel and drapes it over his shoulders. Then he's half guiding, half carrying me to Zeke and Guillermo. "My tough old girl died just before you gunned it. You did that all by yourself." He waves his free hand in the direction of the overturned fence post and the long section of cable stretched across the sand.

"It doesn't matter when the Blazer died." I stop and wait for him to meet my eyes. "I couldn't have . . . I mean . . . I wouldn't have ever done that without you."

He nods and maintains eye contact. We stand like that for several seconds. Then I wrap my arms around his neck and hug him, thankful that he doesn't ask questions or push me away. He seems to understand my desire for silence. I release his neck in favor of his hand.

Zeke beams as we approach. "Good work, kids." He pulls both of us in for a hug, apparently not caring how long it's been since any of us had a shower. Guillermo stands watching from a safe distance.

"Now what?" I ask.

"Guillermo goes back where he belongs. I toss out a bunch

of hay in hopes of drawing the bachelor band this way." He points to the ridge in the distance. "Then we let nature take her course."

"And we head to Manteo?" I ask.

"You and Finn head to Manteo in my truck. I'll stay here and keep an eye on things and go check out the shack if I feel up to it."

Finn and I help Zeke transfer water, hay, and first aid necessities from Franken-truck to the Blazer. The Blazer is pretty much a hollowed-out shell now, but all Zeke needs is a place to rest and store supplies, so it works perfectly for him.

"Catch you on the flip," he says, patting Finn on the back before turning to me. "Thanks, Sophie. You did a good thing."

"You're welcome. I was glad to help." And I was. Rescuing Guillermo gave me a real taste of what it would feel like to be a veterinarian, and it boosted my confidence too. I resolve to talk to Doc Wiggins about creative paths to vet school when things settle down.

After we say our good-byes, Finn and I head for the monster truck. We haven't technically spoken since we were reunited, and I have to say something before I chicken out.

"Uh . . . Finn?"

"Yeah?" He slows down a bit.

"You remember our conversation when we were trying to get your Blazer back on the road?" Of course he remembers. He thinks I shot him down.

"Yes."

"It's not a deal breaker."

He cocks his head, the familiar crease forming between his eyebrows.

"The genetic thing—it's not a deal breaker. I want to be friends . . . or whatever . . ." Heat rises on my neck. I sound like I've reverted to third grade and am communicating through those check-box messages. *Do you like me? Check yes or no or maybe.* "What I'm trying to say is I'm not quitting you."

He squeezes my hand, pulling me to a stop. "Even without guarantees?"

"Even without guarantees . . . and . . ." My palm sweats, but he doesn't seem to notice. Or if he does, it doesn't bother him.

"And?"

"You're *semi*-irresistible." I repeat almost exactly what he suggested I say earlier on the side of the road.

He bursts out laughing. When he pulls me under his arm for a side hug, his whole face lights up, including his dark green eyes. "And sexy?"

"Let's not get too crazy."

"Okay—not *too* crazy." He playfully pokes me in the side. "You ready to hit the road?"

"Beyond ready."

He gestures toward Zeke's truck. "Your carriage awaits."

It's not a glass carriage, and I don't feel like Cinderella. But who needs a carriage when you have an indestructible Franken-truck?

CHAPTER TWENTY-EIGHT

Ring out the false, ring in the true.

ALFRED, LORD TENNYSON

Squinting into the wind blowing through Franken-truck's mesh windows, I study the buildings and landscape as we head south. My mind reels at the stark contrasts. In some places, homes are leveled, stoplights are smashed on the road like Legos, and vehicles are overturned. Then a quarter mile down the road, some random house stands perfectly unscathed, looking out over the surrounding destruction, and asking *what happened?*

Finn's not speeding, or teasing me, or jerking the steering wheel today. He drives well below the speed limit, scanning the road for downed power lines and other dangers. We stick to the main bypass, only detouring if a portion is blocked. The rain has finally stopped, but standing water covers large sections of the road. When we stop at an intersection, there's no wind. It's like Zeke said—things are always changing.

One minute the wind blows, knocking down buildings. The next minute it's drying puddles after the storm. One minute it's blowing families apart. The next it's blowing a handful of random people together, teaching them to work together and opening their eyes to new ways of thinking.

Finn slows almost to a crawl, creeping around a bicycle lying on its side in the middle of the road. We've yet to encounter survivors or emergency personnel. Amid the chaos and destruction in the heart of Kitty Hawk, a flock of seagulls gathers in an empty parking lot—specks of white on a sheet of black asphalt.

"I guess it's a good sign the gulls are back," I say, pointing at the birds.

Finn nods but keeps his eyes glued to the road.

We pass the turn to school, and I wonder how Yesenia weathered the evacuation. She probably made a game out of it, or a party, or used it as an opportunity to check items off her bucket list.

Her bucket list.

Priority number one on her bucket list: Ask someone to the dance.

It would be fun to rock Yesenia's world—to go straight to the top of the list. She may never believe me, but it's worth a shot.

"When do you think we'll go back to school?" I ask, easing myself toward the epic question.

He shrugs. "Maybe next week—you know how islanders are about getting back to business."

The bridge to Manteo comes into view, completely unharmed by the storm of the century, like a tribute to modern-day engineering.

"You're ready to go back to school?" he asks, gripping the steering wheel with two hands. He hugs the side of the road to avoid a downed sign.

"I don't know yet. I guess it depends on Mom and Mere and how much we have to do at the house." I swallow reflexively.

I know Finn likes me. So why is this so terrifying? "Well . . . uh . . . if we have the dance next week, do you want to go?" I just spit it out.

"Huh?"

Franken-truck mounts the bridge and begins her ascent. Whitecaps froth the Albemarle Sound beneath us. If I didn't know better, I'd think we were crossing the ocean, not a shallow coastal inlet.

"Do you . . ." *Spit out the rest, Sophie.* "If we have a dance, do you want to go? With me, I mean?"

Finn stops the truck on the empty bridge. "Really?"

"Really."

He takes one hand off the steering wheel to squeeze my hand. I lace my fingers through his as we start moving again, and just like that we're cresting the bridge and descending. Sandbags and police cruisers block the road into Manteo. The grumpy old guy who was willing to go down with his house would be happy to know the cops are being super conscientious about who gets on the island to ward off looting before it starts. It looks like they're not letting anyone from the mainland onto the islands. Eventually, they'll allow people with proof of residence in areas deemed safe and then go from there. Thankfully, they wave us toward the mainland.

Even though I told Mom I was safe, albeit days ago, and even though she knows cell towers have been out, she must have been worried sick. So seeing her and Mere pressed up against the temporary barriers just past the police cruisers comes as no surprise. I wouldn't put it past her to be the first person to request access across the bridge. My heart soars when I see her messy ponytail and baggy *Horse hair, don't care* sweatshirt.

The small crowd gathered at the blockade watches our approach.

When I step out of Franken-truck, Mom's hands fly to her mouth. I break into a run. Finn follows close behind.

"Sophie! Sophie!" Mere waves. She clutches a sweater to her chest.

Without slowing down, I wave back.

The air whooshes from my lungs when I spot the clean-shaven, bright-eyed man standing behind her. And although his face is pinched with worry, his clothes are clean and his posture straight. I haven't seen this version of Dad in over a year.

My jaw tightens. I'm not prepared for this. I don't know what to say to him or how to act. I slow to a walk. Finn catches up.

"You okay?" he asks, seeming to sense something's not right.

"My dad's here," I say, my voice barely a whisper.

His eyes dart to the onlookers. "Are you good with that?"

"I'm not sure. I think." My eyes lock on Dad's frozen expression. He looks like he might crack down the middle.

Mom barrels toward me, tears streaming down her face. When she grabs me and pulls me against her chest, I lose sight of him.

"I was so worried." She tightens her hold on me.

"I'm fine, Mom." And I am.

Dad hangs several steps behind her, but Mere jumps into the group embrace with more enthusiasm than I've seen from her in a long time. Dad and Finn wait, seeming to understand we need a minute together. When I smile over Mere's shoulder at Finn, he flashes a thumbs-up.

Dad steps forward. His hand lifts as if he's going to touch my shoulder, but he catches himself. "Hi, Soph," he says.

I blink. I've practiced a million cold, spiteful comebacks in hopes that one day I'd have the opportunity to use one of them on him. My lips part, but most of the resentment's gone.

I swallow. "Hi . . . Dad."

I'm not welcoming him home with open arms, but I'm not shutting him out either. Reconciling with an absentee father wasn't exactly on Yesenia's bucket list, but she'd be proud of me anyway for taking the emotional risk.

I pull back from Mom and Mere, motioning Finn forward. "Do y'all remember Finn?"

"Yes! Yes, of course," Mom says.

Mere smiles and nods. Dad stands there, apparently uncertain whether he's part of the *y'all*.

"Finn, this is my family." I gesture toward all three of them.

When I glance over at Finn, a hint of sun breaks through the clouds above his head. It's the first time I've seen the sun in two days. Or is it three?

I've totally lost track of time.

And I'm good with that. In fact, I'm better than good.

I'm perfectly content to lose myself in this moment, surrounded by people I care about. There will be plenty of time tomorrow, and the next day, and the next for clocks, schedules, calendars, and alarms.

Right now, I choose to ride this perfect wave and to enjoy the blush of sun on my cheeks.

I choose my family.

And Finn.

And *kairos*.

CHAPTER TWENTY-NINE

'Tis not too late to seek a newer world.

ALFRED, LORD TENNYSON

It's amazing how the storm of the century shook up our lives. We still have tarps on the barn roof and fences that need to be patched. We lost a good saddle and some other tack. But two weeks after the super storm, the barn, house, and school are mostly back to normal. My physical world suffered damage but nothing that power tools and hard work won't eventually fix. My emotional world, on the other hand, evolved into something completely new and different.

I glance at myself in the full-length mirror, checking to make sure my lip gloss goes with my sleeveless peach dress, completely unembarrassed by the angry bruises and the long scab on my shoulder. In fact, I'm kind of proud of my injury. It's a reminder that no matter how horrible things look in the middle of a storm, chances are the sun will eventually peek out again.

"You look pretty," Mere says from her spot on my bed.

Jim completes a couple of circles on my faded quilt, then curls into a ball at her hip. Mere rests her hand on his head. Smiling, I join them on the edge of the bed.

We sit together in comfortable silence.

The breeze carries Mom's laughter floating in through the open window. She and her friend Carla sit on the front porch, drinking sweet tea and talking about whether to order seafood or Mexican for dinner. Two moms hanging out together on a Friday night might not be a big deal in most families, but it's huge at the March house. Mom seems to be squeezing out of her shell and starting to take some time for herself, to be with friends and get out into the world again instead of just focusing on me and Mere and all our troubles. Of course, she's been super busy putting our lives and the business back together, but I think the hurricane changed Mom too. She told me the storm made her realize she needed to stop focusing on what she lost and start appreciating what she did have. We hugged and cried until the tears on our cheeks ran together, but it was a good cry—the kind that left me feeling hopeful for her. For me. For all of us.

"That's Finn," I say when a car rumbles underneath the house.

Mere nods and scratches Jim behind the ears but makes no effort to leave the comfy spot on my bed. Even she has seemed a little happier these days. I've been wondering if Mere just needed a little room to breathe. Mom and I have been so busy putting the barn and house together that there hasn't been time to fuss over her, and honestly, Mere seems the better for it. She's getting her independence back slowly but surely, something we probably should have helped her do long ago.

"Have fun," she says as I stand to leave.

I smile at her again. "I will." I lean down to give her a quick peck on the check before I head out to meet Finn.

When I grab the Sadie Hawkins dance tickets off the fridge, I see where Mom wrote Dad's number on the calendar for us. She and Dad have been texting and talking on the phone. He hasn't been home. None of us are ready for that, but it's good to know where he is, how he's doing, and that if we reach out in an emergency, he'll be there. When she contacted him about my being stranded on the island, he drove down from Virginia and immediately started organizing people to look for me. Thankfully, it hadn't come to that.

"Hey, you look good, Bookworm," Finn says when I step out on the deck.

The ocean breeze brushes my hair and face. The high temperatures finally broke after the storm, and the cool air feels nice on the heat rising on my cheeks. After a long pause, I find my voice. "You too, Finn."

And he does look really good. His black hair is shorter now and perfectly frames his eyes, making their green pop against his tan skin and highlighting the strength of his nose.

Mom and Carla stare at us all starry-eyed, like they're remembering high school dances of their own.

"Have fun," Mom says without standing. "And be careful."

"We will," Finn says, lacing his fingers through mine.

And we will. Finn's still Finn, thank goodness. But it seems like the storm or our time together has affected him as well. For one thing, he keeps his mom's car, which he's been driving since the storm, cleaner than he ever kept his own. For another, he's been trying to eat a little better—at least when we're together.

I lean down to give Mom a kiss too before following him to his car.

"You think Yesenia will be ready?" he asks as he holds the door open for me.

"Probably. She's pretty excited. And Alex was supposed to be at her house an hour ago." But then Yesenia's always pretty excited, especially when she can mark something huge off the bucket list, like inviting dates to the Sadie Hawkins dance.

I smile at recent additions to the front seat. Finn has tucked his duct-taped *Don't Sweat the Small Stuff* book in the compartment holders between the seats and a water bottle instead of a soda in the cup holder.

As he walks around to his side, I inhale deeply and relax against the headrest. The sun sets behind the barn in a kaleidoscope of reds and fuchsias, signaling a beautiful end to the day and hinting at the possibility of tomorrow.

And I remind myself to tell Yesenia about the Tennyson quote I found when I was studying earlier today. I'm surprised she's never used it on me. I wrote it in the notes on my phone and plan to live by it this year—*'Tis not too late to seek a newer world.*

She'll like it. I know I do. Even though I don't know exactly what the future holds, I've learned that I can't control everything. And that's okay. But I've also learned I don't have to compromise my dreams.

As Finn slides into the driver's seat and reaches for my hand, I promise myself I'll continue to chase those dreams, whether that's tonight at this dance, in my relationships with the people I care about, or even at vet school if that's what's meant to be.

An ocean-size smile stretches my face when I realize I'm starting to believe in happily-ever-afters after all.

Acknowledgments

I couldn't write without my patient and supportive family. They love me despite this roller coaster ride of publishing books. Thanks especially to my mom and husband but also to my children, my sister and brother, my stepfather, my in-laws, and all the rest. You know who you are. If you've listened to me talk about writing or come to a book event, I'm talking to you.

Thanks also to Laura Baker, one of the best writing coaches on the face of the planet. Her Discovering Story Magic lessons on character development and emotion always push me out of my comfort zone.

A huge thanks to my student and teacher friends, and especially to my principal, Suzanne Jarrard, who allowed me to teach part-time so I could write and revise all the words, and to Alan Arena, who read for me and talked plot.

Thanks to two of my best friends, who run and walk with me, albeit very slowly. Laurie Brown and Joy Parham have learned more about the business of writing and publishing than I'm sure they ever wanted or intended.

No writer could make it without her tribe, so thanks to my ever-growing circle of writing friends, my 2014 and 2016 Golden Heart Award sisters; my dear friends and critique partners, Holly Bodger and Kim McCarron; and especially Amy DeLuca, my critique partner and kindred spirit.

And of course, thanks to my dream agent, Amanda Leuck, and my dream editor, Jillian Manning. Without their belief in Sophie and her story, this book would not be possible.

Discussion Questions
for Meet the Sky

1. At the beginning of the book, Sophie avoids risks at all costs. Finn confronts them head-on. Which do you think is the healthier way to approach risk-taking? Why?

2. Alfred Lord Tennyson once said, "'Tis better to have loved and lost than never to have loved at all." Do you agree or disagree? Why?

3. As she and Finn experience the worsening storm together, Sophie gradually learns to give up control. When is a time you pushed yourself out of your comfort zone and gave up trying to control a situation? How did it work out for you? If you could, would you change how you handled the situation? Why or why not?

4. Each of the chapters opens with an epigraph—a line of Tennyson poetry. Which line spoke to you the most? Explain.

5. As an English teacher and a reader, I love symbolism. I love looking for hidden messages in the world around me. Did you notice any symbolism or motifs in *Meet*

the Sky? How did they add additional depth to the story?

6. If you didn't notice any symbolism or motifs, think about and discuss what symbols you might have used in *Meet the Sky* or in any story about learning to take risks.

7. All good stories are about dynamic characters that grow and change. What character do you think grows the most? Explain.

8. Obviously, the overriding theme of Sophie's story is one of learning to take risks, but there are several other underlying themes about the human spirit. What other themes did you notice, and how did they apply to you or the world around you?

9. How important do you think the setting of *Meet the Sky* is to Sophie's story? Would she be the same person and learn the same lessons without the Outer Banks and the hurricane? How does when and where you live affect all aspects of your life?

10. How important is Finn to Sophie's story? Would she have grown and learned the same lessons with another person? What sorts of people have you surrounded yourself with, and how do they affect your actions and emotions?

Interview with McCall Hoyle

1) **This is now your second book. How was writing _Meet the Sky_ a different experience from writing _The Thing with Feathers_?**

In _The Thing with Feathers_, most of the conflicts were internal issues that Emilie was struggling to overcome. There was danger, but it was mostly emotional danger. In _Meet the Sky_, Sophie is dealing with internal struggles and conflicts, but she's also got a hurricane to contend with and the whole issue of being stranded with a guy she doesn't like very much. The stories are very different, but I love them both and hope readers will too.

2) **Sophie is a girl who is carrying a lot of burdens in her life—watching over the family business, caring for her sister, and dealing with feelings of rejection after her dad left and Finn stood her up at her dance. And in many ways, she's allowed the past to shape her future. What inspired her character? And what do you hope readers take away from her story?**

My father died unexpectedly when I was thirty. For several years, I was emotionally paralyzed by grief. I went about the business of living and raising my family and teaching, but I was frozen on the inside. Eventually, I was able to process a lot of my grief through writing. I never would have wanted to lose my dad so unexpectedly, but I learned a lot of important lessons about living every moment to the fullest and about opening my heart to others and taking risks. I want readers to think about how they can live their own lives to the fullest and embrace every day and all its ups and downs.

3) **Throughout *Meet the Sky*, the poetry of Tennyson makes an appearance, and Yesenia's favorite quote, "'Tis better to have loved and lost than never to have loved at all," plays a part in Sophie's decision to take some risks. What drew you to Tennyson's work, and how much did the quotes help shape the book, or vice versa?**

All the Tennyson epigraphs in the book are important, but it was really that one line that started the whole story. As I mentioned earlier, losing my father was the one event that has shaped my life more than any other. My dad was all about taking risks and trying new things. He was not afraid to fail and get back up again. He was brave—a lot like Finn. I think we can learn a lot from people like that, especially if we tend to be a bit reticent and want to try to control everything—pointing to self here. And I think Tennyson's quotation is about more than just taking risks in love. I think it's about taking risks in general.

4) **Like Sophie, you once lived in the Outer Banks of North Carolina. Can you share a little about that experience, and what drew you to use the setting in each of your books so far?**

The Outer Banks is the most ruggedly beautiful place I've ever lived or visited. The narrow strips of land that could have, maybe even should have, been wiped out by hurricanes and Nor' easters always weather the storms. There

248

is something in the resilience of the place and its people that draws me back again and again

5) **Did you ever experience a hurricane or storm while you lived in North Carolina? If so, what was the experience like?**

I lived on the Outer Banks of North Carolina after graduating from college. I was newly married at the time. Mostly, I'm a scaredy cat, so we generally evacuated long before a storm made landfall. e did stay on the island for a Category One torm. The powerful force of nature was both terrifying and awe-inspiring, and that was during a minimal storm. I cannot imagine being on an island in an even more powerful storm.

6) **While he makes a brief appearance, Jim the cat is a very special feline in the book. Can you tell us more about him, and what inspired you to place him in the book?**

I am an animal lover and strongly believe we have much to learn about being better humans from animals. Jim is based on a cat that adopted my family. I often contemplate his amazingness. He is the true definition of a survivor. That little cat with his three-and-a-half legs has been through a lot of trauma. His horrific past could have made him really skittish, but it didn't. He is the most trusting and content creature I've ever met, and he knows how to live in the moment. I think there is a really important lesson in there for most of us.

7) **Now for some fun questions. What things would you write down if you made a bucket list? Are there any items you feel you've already crossed off that list?**

Some things I've always wanted to do but haven't had

the time or the opportunity yet are: hike the Appalachian Trail, see grizzly bears in the wild, visit Alaska, compete with my dog in agility competitions, read the Bible cover-to-cover without skipping around.

Some things I've actually checked off are: finishing a marathon and publishing a book.

8) **If you were stuck inside a closet during a bad storm, what would you grab to keep yourself entertained while you waited out the weather?**

Easy. Books and a book light.

9) **What is your favorite part about being an author?**

Hands down, the best part of being an author is seeing my books in the hands of my own high school and middle school students. A very, very close second is meeting new readers, teachers, and librarians and talking about books and the world.

10) **Finally, what are you working on next?**

I have so many ideas right now. I'm trying to narrow down the list. I feel certain readers can count on an uplifting story about a teenage girl who is either braver or stronger than she originally thinks.

Emilie Day believes in playing it safe: she's homeschooled, her best friend is her seizure dog, and she's probably the only girl on the Outer Banks of North Carolina who can't swim.

Then Emilie's mom enrolls her in public school, and Emilie goes from studying at home in her pj's to halls full of strangers. To make matters worse, Emilie is paired with starting point guard Chatham York for a major research project on Emily Dickinson. She should be ecstatic when Chatham shows interest, but she has a problem. She hasn't told anyone about her epilepsy.

Emilie lives in fear her recently adjusted meds will fail and she'll seize at school. Eventually, the worst happens, and she must decide whether to withdraw to safety or follow a dead poet's advice and "dwell in possibility."

From Golden Heart award-winning author McCall Hoyle comes *The Thing with Feathers*, a story of overcoming fears, forging new friendships, and finding a first love, perfect for fans of Jennifer Niven, Robyn Schneider, and Sharon M. Draper.

Available now wherever books are sold!

BLINK

About the Author

McCall Hoyle writes honest YA novels about friendship, first love, and girls finding the strength to overcome great challenges. She is a high school English teacher. Her own less-than-perfect teenage experiences and those of the girls she teaches inspire many of the struggles in her books. When she's not reading or writing, she's spending time with her family and their odd assortment of pets—a food-obsessed beagle, a grumpy rescue cat, and a three-and-a-half-legged kitten. She has an English degree from Columbia College and a master's degree from Georgia State University. She lives in a cottage in the woods in North Georgia, where she reads and writes every day. Learn more at mcallhoyle.com.

 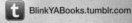